One Dead, Two to Go

One Dead, Two to Go

An Eddie Shoes Mystery

———•———

Elena Hartwell

Seattle, WA

CAMEL
PRESS

Camel Press
PO Box 70515
Seattle, WA 98127

For more information go to: www.camelpress.com
www.elenahartwell.com

Cover design by Sabrina Sun

One Dead, Two to Go
Copyright © 2016 by Elena Hartwell

ISBN: 978-1-60381-311-2 (Trade Paper)
ISBN: 978-1-60381-312-9 (eBook)

Library of Congress Control Number: 2015953092

Printed in the United States of America

With love to Sherry L. Hartwell.

I'm so lucky you're my mom.

———•———

Acknowledgments

———•———

To my best friend and husband John "JD" Hammerly, who came up with the name Eddie Shoes. *Who is this Eddie Shoes?* I asked myself, and now I know. To the amazing Jennifer McCord, Catherine Treadgold, and all the people at Coffeetown and Camel Press for their hard work and support in making this book happen. To the Issaquah Police Department and Detective Diego Zanella, who gave so generously of his time to answer my questions and provide me with insights into the real world of homicide investigation. Any mistake in police procedure is because I didn't ask the right question. To my beta reader Janice Schwarz for her thoughtful feedback on my work. And to Andrea Karin Nelson, who keeps me writing. So lucky to have had you as a writing partner all these years, can't wait to see what the future brings us.

Chapter One

———•———

CALL ME EDDIE SHOES. NOT a very feminine moniker, but it suits me. My father's name was Eduardo Zapata. My mother, Chava, in a fit of nostalgia, named me Edwina Zapata Schultz, even though by the time I was born she hadn't seen my father in seven months. Edwina was a mouthful to saddle any child with, and at the ripe old age of six, I announced to Chava I would only answer to Eddie. I didn't have any nostalgia for a guy I'd never met, so Zapata just seemed like a name no one ever spelled right the first time. I also didn't care much for Schultz, and Chava wasn't particularly maternal in any conventional sense, so not a lot of nostalgia there either. At eighteen I legally changed my name to Eddie Shoes.

That said a lot about my sense of humor.

Chava and I had come to an understanding. I kept her in my life as long as our contact was minimal and primarily over email. It was just enough to allay her guilt and not enough to make me crazy, so it worked out for both of us. She'd always been down on my choice of career, but what did she expect from a girl who called herself Eddie Shoes? If I hadn't become a private investigator, I probably would have been a bookie, so

I figured she should have been a little more positive about the whole thing.

My career was the reason I sat hunkered in the car, in the dark, halfway down the block from a tacky hotel, clutching a digital camera and zoom lens, waiting to catch my latest client's husband with a woman not his wife. I'd already gotten a few choice shots of the guy entering the room, but he'd gone in alone and no one else had arrived, so I assumed the other woman was already waiting for him. I'd been tailing the guy for a few days, so I had a pretty good guess who the chippie would turn out to be. I didn't think he'd hired his "office manager" for her filing skills, and sleeping with the married boss was a cliché because it happened all the time. I could already prove the man a liar. He told his wife he played poker with the boys on Wednesday nights, and I didn't think he was shacked up in this dive with three of his closest buddies, unless he was kinkier than I imagined.

But then, people never ceased to amaze me.

December in Bellingham, Washington, often brought cold, clear weather and that night was no exception. Starting the engine to warm up sounded tempting, but I didn't want anyone to notice me sitting there. Nice it wasn't raining, but if the thermometer crept much over twenty, I hadn't noticed. To make matters worse, my almost six-foot frame had been scrunched down in the driver's seat for more than two hours. Even with a blanket wrapped around my shoulders, I was half frozen, and I desperately hoped my mark didn't have more stamina than I'd pegged him for. All I wanted was to go home and go to bed.

And at some point I would need to pee.

Finally, up on the second floor, the door of the hotel room I had my eye on opened. I brought my camera up, ready for the money shots. I knew from my earlier pics that the dirty white stucco on the side of the building bounced the pale glow from the minimal exterior lights enough for my pictures to be clear without a flash. Even from a distance, I had a nice, unobstructed view of the location. The only barrier between someone standing on the narrow walk and my camera lens was a flimsy, rusty-looking, wrought-iron railing. The balusters looked too thin to stop anyone from falling the height of the first floor to the asphalt parking lot below, and I wondered if anything at the tawdry place passed code.

I wasn't going to stay there, so what did I care?

The "liar"—I have always been creative with nicknames—stepped out, straightening his tie. I snapped a few pictures and held my breath, hoping the other woman would come out behind him. Even if I took pictures of her exiting a few minutes later, I needed the husband in the picture with her. Otherwise, a surprising number of wives would argue with me about what actually took place in these various, if interchangeable, hotel rooms. For some reason they would rather believe I faked the info about their husband cheating than admit he strayed, which confused me because I got paid either way. It seemed especially crazy when you considered that they must already know the truth, given they hired me in the first place. But I knew better than to look for logic in the ways of the human heart. I got the best evidence possible.

The man turned, his face silhouetted by the light coming from the room behind him. He had an exceptionally generous head of hair, which made him quite recognizable, even in bad light. Mid-forties, and mostly in good shape, he appeared athletic as long as he didn't unbutton his sports coat. I could see why women were attracted to him, though he didn't do a thing for me. I liked my men a little more honest.

But then, I'd never been married, so what did I know?

A figure moved from behind him into the shadow of the doorway.

"Come on, honey, step out into the light," I said, holding the camera up to my eye. "One more step, so I can see your face."

The woman obliged by leaning into the cold blue glow

thrown by the old style, energy inefficient streetlights, her cheeks stained red in the flash of the vacancy sign. I happily clicked away as the "office manager" wrapped her arms around his neck and whispered sweet nothings in his ear. She clearly wore nothing but lingerie. I guess she assumed no one else would be out this late on such a cold weeknight. Or maybe she enjoyed having people see her, a bit of an exhibitionist of the happy home-wrecker variety. Whatever the cause, she had him in the perfect spot for the best pictures.

I loved it when guilty people made my job easy.

My photos might not be art, but they were gold in my book. No way the wife could believe this was anything but what it looked like.

I clicked away until the husband extricated himself from the mistress and she ducked back into the room and closed the door. Then he walked briskly toward a shiny red Chevy Camaro—the guy owned a GM dealership and drove a new car every day. He lit a cigarette, which he puffed on for a few drags before he tossed it into the gutter. Not just a cheater, but also a litterer, the bastard. The cigarette stench backed his poker party story and covered the smell of another woman, killing two birds with one cancer-causing stone.

As soon as he pulled out onto the street, I stretched back up to full height, relieved I could still feel my feet. I started up my ancient green Subaru Forester, cranked my heater, and headed for home, relieved I didn't have to wait around in the cold for the mistress to reappear. Whatever she did next wasn't my concern. Having the two of them in the pictures together convinced me my work was done.

The hotel was located downtown—the blue collar north end, not the high-priced, brick, historical south end, so I dropped down to Lakeway Drive, scooted under the freeway, and wound through the streets, which curved around Bayview Cemetery. Traffic at 10:00 on a midweek winter night was light, and I arrived at my little house by 10:30. I downloaded the photos from the hotel onto my computer, wrote up a final bill for my client, and went to bed content. What could possibly go wrong with such an easy case?

Chapter Two

———•———

After my late night activities, I celebrated by sleeping in past 7:30. With no alarm clock shrieking for my attention, I enjoyed a few extra, luxurious moments in bed. I considered texting my client for a meeting, but decided to hold off until I'd gotten myself fully awake. Heading to the kitchen, I turned on my coffee pot and contemplated Kendra Hallings. Dealing with angry wives can be a lot of work, but it beat dealing with angry husbands. I don't take on angry husbands as clients. I did that once when I first started out on my own, but after receiving incontrovertible proof that his wife had cheated on him, the fathead tried to kill her.

That kind of took the fun out of things for me.

I decided right then and there to stick to female clients when it involved cheating spouses. They were less likely to go postal on their wayward hubbies. They went for the jugular, but usually not in a literal sense, more in a financial one.

After fortifying myself with coffee and cornflakes, I decided it was time to face the music. Kendra had already proven herself to be a crier—she could turn on the waterworks quicker than a soap opera diva—so I wasn't looking forward to delivering her the news her wifely instincts were correct. I stripped off my nightshirt and pulled on a pair of jeans and a t-shirt, layering it with a plaid, flannel shirt from the Cabela's Sporting Goods catalog and a North Face jacket. I tried to buy all my clothes online or from Costco. It cut down on trips to malls, boutique stores, and other places that gave me hives.

Sufficiently bundled for the weather, I grabbed my camera and laptop and headed over to my home away from home. My office was in a free-standing building between the historic Fairhaven neighborhood and downtown to the north. With a population of just over 80,000, Bellingham—or B'ham as we abbreviate it around here—wasn't exactly a sprawling metropolis. Driving across town didn't produce the headache it might in places like Seattle or Tokyo or Syracuse, so when I bought my house, I hadn't worried too much about the commute.

Buying a house without a view of Bellingham Bay also saved me a big chunk of change. I loved the water views much of my town afforded, but given my income, I had to settle for a view of the trees and bushes in my backyard. Lookout Mountain was visible from my driveway, so that counted for something. A tiny trickle of water also ran along the east side of my property. During spring rains and snowmelt it could probably be called a creek.

Which is almost as good as a waterfront view, right?

My office wasn't much to look at either, but it was mine, and that counted for a lot in my book. It had easy access to the freeway, Fairhaven, and downtown, complete with the waterfront and multiple tattoo parlors. I'd never had call to use the services of the latter, but you never know, it could happen. I was also very close to Rocket Donuts, with their distinctive aluminum rocket ship in the parking lot. And who doesn't love donuts and sci-fi mixed together under one roof?

One of the best things about my office was a small parking lot with a second entrance at the back of the building. My clients could come and go without being seen from the street. There was no big sign announcing my services—private investigators don't usually get work from foot traffic. My office maintained a certain anonymity. When I first started out on my own, I thought about installing an espresso machine to get people in the door, but PI and Espresso sounded a little hokey. I'm not sure anyone else would have found it strange here in the coffee capitol of the United States but "Do you want extra foam with your background check?" seemed a bit much. Luckily, I managed to stay afloat without adding barista to my résumé.

Probably a good thing, given I drank too much coffee already and I would have sucked down most of my profits.

No other cars were in the parking lot this early in the morning. The business currently sharing the building with me was questionable. Their hours were even more erratic than mine, but at least they were quiet. The sign in the window read "Tarot," but I had a feeling the young women who came and went there didn't actually read cards so much as provide happy endings. I guess good fortune was all in how you thought about it. The "employees" might not be able to predict anyone's future, but at least they provided an actual service.

The setup of the building created a lot of privacy for our respective clients. A hallway split the building in half, so we didn't share any walls. From the street, my office was on the left and the "Fortune Tellers" were on the right. Both offices had small kitchenettes and private bathrooms attached, and given the reasonable rent, I didn't care if they were making crack cocaine next door as long as they didn't burn the building down.

I unlocked both outside doors, the one to the street in front and the parking lot in back, anticipating I'd be calling my client to come down. Then I unlocked and entered my own office. Pausing momentarily, I admired the EDDIE SHOES, PRIVATE INVESTIGATOR sign painted in black and gold lettering on the frosted glass of my interior office door before I slipped inside, just because it made me happy.

It was often the simple things in life that brightened my day, so I tried hard not to overlook them.

Sitting behind my desk, I pulled out a drawer, where my active files were easily accessible. They'd get archived in the locking filing cabinets behind my desk after I finished with them and stored for seven years before being converted to an ash pile. Or at least that was the plan. I hadn't actually been in business long enough to permanently dispose of anything yet. Pulling out my file on Mrs. Kendra T. Hallings, I decided to make coffee before contacting her. I hadn't had quite enough caffeine at home.

Before I could reach my coffee maker, my office phone rang. My cell could handle all my calls, but I also had a good, old-fashioned landline I couldn't quite get myself to give up. I knew I didn't have to pay for the cost of one, but something about that black, Bakelite antique perched on my desk symbolized that I had made it on my own. I had an office and a phone. Who could argue with success like that? Besides, I loved the little clicky sounds the rotary phone made when the dial spun. Sometimes, when I was bored, I practiced answering the phone in my best Humphrey Bogart imitation à la Philip Marlowe.

So far I hadn't answered an actual call that way, but maybe next year for Halloween.

It was also the only thing I'd taken with me from the office I'd shared with my mentor, Benjamin Cooper. It comforted me that my hand now rested where his had for so many years, even though he'd died the way he had.

Picking up after the second ring, I answered in my professional voice. It was my client, sounding like she might be hyperventilating.

"Eddie? It's me, Kendra. I tried your cellphone, but it went straight to voicemail, so I thought I'd try your office. I'm just wondering if you have anything for me yet."

"Hi, Kendra, I was just about to call you." Pulling out my

cellphone, I realized I'd left it silenced from the night before. Clicking the button on the side, I turned my ringer back on. The little voicemail icon showed only the one call from Kendra.

"Good news or bad?" she asked.

Jeez, how should I answer that?

"Can you come over to my office?" I asked instead of answering her.

There was a pause on the other end of the line.

"Was I right?" she said, her voice small and tremulous.

"I think we should talk through things in person," I said, reminding myself she deserved sympathy for her situation, even if I did think she'd be better off dumping the lout.

"Really?" Kendra asked, or at least that's what I thought she said between sobs.

"Do you think you can pull yourself together? You sound upset."

"I'm …"—hiccup—"I'm …"—sob—"okay."

I waited, listening to her breathe in and out a few times. Her deep breathing sounded like the kind you might be taught to do in meditation or yoga.

"Yes," she said after much huffing and puffing, her voice stronger, "but I can't be there until later this afternoon. I have some things I need to do. Will three o'clock work for you?"

I assured her it would and she hung up before I could give her a "You go, girl," which was probably just as well. She might have heard it as sarcasm. I plugged in my computer to organize the latest photos, downloaded the night before. I'd already set up a slideshow to ease Kendra into the situation, starting with shots of her husband at the dealership with the office manager in the background. Nothing overt, but I wanted my client to have the woman's face in her mind when she saw the photos from the hotel. I had known there would be a hotel.

There was always a hotel.

I finished the slideshow by adding the pictures of her husband pulling up in front and then him leaving a few hours later along with the shots of the mistress kissing him goodbye.

The guy really did have great hair.

Voices sounded in the hallway. I thought perhaps Kendra had arrived early and brought a friend for moral support. I opened the door before they knocked, surprising a man with his arm raised. He had turned away, so I was lucky he didn't tap, tap, tap on my chest before he realized the door no longer stood in front of him. Even in profile, however, I would have recognized him. I'd last seen him almost two years ago, before I left Seattle after Coop died. In a panic, I did the only thing that made sense in the moment.

I slammed the door in his face.

Chapter Three

————•————

THE LOUD POUNDING SHOULDN'T HAVE come as a surprise. After all, the police weren't used to people slamming doors in their faces, and that's who I'd just locked out of my office.

"Eddie? What the—? Open the door." Chance Parker's voice hadn't changed. It was still low, but carried a weight to it like every word he spoke mattered. I leaned against the glass with the hope my heart wouldn't leap out of my chest and splatter on the ground at my, or worse yet *his*, feet.

The next rap was a knuckle on the glass, instead of the wood frame of the door. The sharp sound of it pulled me out of my panic, and I wrenched the door back open. Just like ripping off a bandage, best to get it over with quick.

"Sorry about that. I thought I heard the phone ring," I said, my response inexplicable even to myself.

The woman with Chance looked at me like I might be certifiable; he just looked amused. I'm not sure which expression annoyed me more.

"Mind if we come in? We have a few questions for you," Chance said, though it was clear he wasn't going to take no for an answer. The "we" included Detective Kate Jarek, who introduced herself and said, "I understand you two know each other."

"We do," I said, looking to Chance to see if he planned to fill me in on what he'd told her about our history.

Chance rubbed the side of his cheek as if checking for stubble. It was an action I remembered well—an unconscious gesture he made when he didn't know exactly how he wanted to respond. Chance was careful with his words, as if they were valuable and he might accidentally drop one he couldn't afford to lose.

"Down in Seattle," he said. His eyes held mine, and for an instant I thought he might say more. Something was there in the softness of his gaze, but that brief moment of connection passed and he glossed over a complicated relationship with that single sentence.

I told myself he couldn't do anything else. Even if it might have felt good to hear he forgave me, now wasn't the time.

Maybe we could see each other again soon. Alone. And I could find a way to make amends.

"Come on in," I said, standing aside to let the two of them through the door. I shut it behind them, taking a deep breath before I turned around to face them.

Chance began to pace, his nervous energy filling the room. From the way he averted his gaze from the two of us, I could tell his mind was now focused solely on whatever brought him to my door. I respected that about him. His attention would be directed at you for a moment—intense, all consuming—then he'd turn outward again, as his work took precedence.

Chance was taller than Kate by at least six inches. I could look him in the eye if I were wearing tall shoes, so he stood just over six feet. His hair was brown, but if we were outside, sunlight would glint off red highlights. His eyes were the color of dark chocolate—that satiny look it took on when you melted it on the stove to make some delicious, fattening dessert you knew you shouldn't eat but couldn't help yourself from making.

"What can I do for you?" I asked, curious about why a Seattle detective—and my old flame—had appeared on my doorstep up here in Bellingham.

"We've got some questions about Deirdre Fox," Kate said.

That certainly threw me for a loop. I don't know what I thought they might question me about, but Deirdre Fox wasn't even in the top ten.

"Okay," I said, wanting to see where their questions would lead.

"Were you following her or working for her?" Chance asked, confusing me even further.

"Neither," I said, which was technically true.

"Care to explain this?" Kate handed me a photo that looked like a still picture taken from a video surveillance camera. It wasn't very high quality, but it was good enough to identify me in my Subaru taking pictures with my telephoto lens. I could tell from the background it was from my stakeout at Hallings' dealership.

"Why would you think I was tailing Deirdre?" Maybe the woman had filed a report she was being stalked and my name had come up as the stalker.

Maybe I wasn't as stealthy as I thought.

"Because she turned up dead this morning," Chance said, carefully gauging my reaction. Shock kept me quiet and he continued, "In recreating her final day, we scanned the videotapes from her place of business, looking for anything unusual. Then you showed up." Chance tilted his head in that way he had, eyes narrowed, reading your every move, like a cat getting ready to pounce.

"*Dead*?" I repeated, trying to absorb the fact that someone I saw yesterday in her lingerie was no longer breathing.

"Dead." Kate said.

"Accidental?" I asked, thinking maybe she had fallen over that flimsy railing. But I got no reply save the flat stares of two homicide detectives.

Maybe that was my answer.

"Dead when?" A tight, clenched feeling started in my gut. The memory of Chance Parker telling me about another person, dead by his own hand, rose in my mind. "Dead how?"

The two detectives exchanged a glance, and I felt a stir of jealousy. They had the ability to communicate silently, in a way only old married couples and police partnered in the field are able to do.

"Tell me this wasn't a suicide," I said. Chance shook his head, as Benjamin Cooper's ghost rose up between us. He shot a nod to Kate.

"Not a suicide," Kate said as the two of them decided via telepathy to give me some information, at least about the time of death, or TOD as the police would say. "We think she died between ten and midnight last night."

Ten o'clock would mean she died right after I'd taken pictures of her. I hoped that didn't mean I was a suspect if this was a murder. Had I been the last person to see her alive?

Should I have noticed something?

I did some quick calculations. I'd left the hotel right around 10:00, with Deirdre Fox alive and well, and hopefully basking in the post-coital glow of her romp with Matthew Hallings. Hallings left before I did, but he could have returned later instead of going home. Then there was my client. Was she capable of violence? Had she followed me? Had I led her right to the mistress? She didn't appear the type for that kind of act, but what did we ever really know about another human being?

For the moment, neither one was off the table for Deirdre's death.

Neither was I, for that matter, when it came to alibis.

"I'll tell you what I know," I said, filling them in on my investigation into Hallings, his affair with Deirdre, and how I'd last seen her at the hotel during the TOD the police had established. Private Investigators had a code of conduct, but we weren't bound by confidentiality like an attorney. I wouldn't intentionally throw Kendra under the bus, but I had a responsibility to the law.

"You're sure about what time you saw Matthew Hallings leave the hotel?" Chance said when I was done. "With Deirdre still alive?"

I nodded.

Had she died at the hotel?

"What can you tell us about the wife?" Kate asked.

"She's petite," I said, wondering if Deirdre died from the kind of trauma that would require more strength than my client would be physically able to inflict. "Early thirties. So far she's been a crier, but I haven't seen her angry yet about her suspicions of the affair, so I can't tell you if she would go into a killing rampage, if this is a homicide we're talking about …." I left the door open for them to fill in the blank, but neither one stepped over the threshold.

"Suspicions?" Chance said. "You haven't given her proof?"

"She's coming by later this afternoon. She said she had things to do until then."

"We'll need copies of all the photos you took that included Deirdre," Chance said. I was guessing there hadn't been any surveillance cameras outside the hotel, so my photos would be the only photographic evidence they'd have from there. I nodded. Taking a memory stick from the top drawer of my desk, I made sure it was empty and downloaded the photos from the dealership and the hotel.

"This is the camera," I said as I got out my digital and showed Kate that it registered the correct time stamp.

Kate made a note.

"Your IT people can prove I was online at home about eleven," I said, still wondering if I needed an alibi. Should I worry that I had a whole unaccounted-for hour overlapping with the official TOD?

"So you didn't see anyone else? Following Deirdre? Or at the hotel?" Kate said in a tone of voice that felt like disapproval.

Was I supposed to have known she was in danger? There was that tug of guilt again.

"No. But keep in mind it wasn't Deirdre I was following; it was Hallings."

"Right."

What was *that* supposed to mean? I could feel a lump lodge in my chest and I resented it. Deirdre's death wasn't my responsibility any more than Benjamin Cooper's was, yet somehow I felt like I should have seen something that would have helped.

"You couldn't have known what would happen," Chance said.

Was he talking about Deirdre? Or Coop?

Kate looked surprised, though at his comment or my reaction I wasn't sure.

"No," she said. "Of course, I didn't mean it that way."

Her tone didn't convince me, but at least Deirdre wasn't a suicide. One suicide on my conscience was enough.

Kate handed me a business card. "We'll be in touch if we have more questions."

"Where did you find her?" I asked, assuming it had to be somewhere public for them to be this far into their investigation. Had she died at that hotel? Right after I drove away?

"It's going to be on the news," Chance said, looking at Kate and answering a question she hadn't asked. "She'll put two and two together."

"Her body was found in an abandoned building around three o'clock this morning," Kate said.

"Found by whom?"

"We believe it was tweakers who'd gone in to pull out the wiring."

Meth addicts had taken to removing copper wiring from buildings to sell for drug money. It was bad enough when they stripped old, abandoned buildings, where the power was off, but every once in awhile they went after live wires and ended up fried for their troubles.

"She was stuffed behind a crawlspace. If it weren't for the anonymous tip the tweakers gave us, she might never have been found," Kate said.

"You're moving fast on this," I said, noting that she'd only been discovered a few hours ago.

"Plain view," Kate said, meaning the body could be seen without entering the building, which would have sped up getting inside. "The tweakers had pulled her into the front room, so her foot was visible through the window. The patrol officer who arrived on the scene went in to see about resuscitation, but it was clear she was dead."

"I had the search warrant on the judge's doorstep before five a.m.," Chance said, shaking his head at the memory. "Not a great way to meet a local judge for the first time, but she knows the drill."

Once the police knew Deirdre couldn't be revived, they would have to wait for a search warrant before starting their investigation. The patrolman would have immediately exited the building, called for backup, and secured the premises.

"She had ID on her?" I asked, surprised that someone would hide a body but leave a way to identify the corpse.

"The ME had just bought a new Chevy," Chance said, referencing the medical examiner who would have been first on the scene. Even the detectives couldn't touch her until the ME had finished his job. "Deirdre had done his paperwork. He recognized her."

Bad luck for whoever stuck her in the wall, but good luck for Deirdre. Or at least, good luck toward finding her killer. The first twenty-four hours were the most important in a homicide investigation. The fact the detectives found the body and were able to get inside the building and ID her so fast could be invaluable.

"We'd appreciate it if you'd keep that part of her death to yourself for the time being," Chance said as the two started to depart. "She won't be identified on the news." He made it sound like a request, but I knew the truth. Interfering with their investigation would get me into serious trouble. I could mention Deirdre's death to my client, but not the circumstances.

"Chance, wait," I said, enjoying the feel of his name on my tongue. "What are you doing here, in Bellingham?"

"Bellingham had a spot open. I transferred in."

"James Mallory?" I asked, turning to Kate, who nodded.

The Bellingham Police Department had a number of detectives working in their Major Crimes Task Force, including James Mallory, who'd had to take time off to deal with ailing parents. The rest of the team had been working additional hours to cover his absence.

"He left permanently?" I'd worked with him a year or so ago on a domestic abuse situation and liked him.

"His father died and he's decided to help his mother move to Florida," Kate filled me in. "He said he wouldn't mind a little more sun."

The weather here in the Pacific Northwest wasn't for everyone.

"I'm sorry to hear about his father," I said, then turned to Chance again, "Will you let me know what you find?" Chance shrugged, and I knew him well enough to understand he'd chosen not to respond, not that he didn't have an answer. I let it go and the two headed for the door.

"Nice to see you, Eddie," he said, just before he slipped out, a smile lighting his face. It was the look that always got me. That little moment when you felt his attention solely on you and knew he liked it that way too.

"We should find a time to catch up," I said, ignoring the pleading undertone of my voice.

"Right now I'm a little tied up," he said.

Then he was gone.

I knew it wasn't personal. When detectives are on a homicide case, the investigation consumes all their time. The two lead detectives work until they get so tired they might make a mistake, then after a few hours to recharge they are right back at it. That can go on for a very long time.

But it felt personal.

My heart hadn't stopped racing since I'd first seen Chance Parker in the hall, but now it felt like it might never beat again. I'd extended an olive branch. Had it just been refused? Or merely delayed?

Before I could get myself too twisted into a knot trying to analyze Chance's reaction, a knock sounded on my door.

"Come on in," I called out, thinking the police had forgotten a question. But the person stepping into my office wasn't Bellingham's finest.

"Crap," I said, "what are you doing here?"

Chapter Four

———•———

"That's no way to greet your mother," Chava Ester Schultz said as she filled my office doorway. Stunned, I watched her sweep through the door rolling a rather large piece of luggage, followed by a second, larger piece of luggage, strapped to the first like a dog on a chain. She also carried a handbag big enough to house most of a circus act and a brown paper grocery bag I suspected might contain actual groceries.

"Chava," I repeated, "what are you doing here?"

"Visiting you." She set down her various accouterments and came around the side of my desk for a hug.

My mother was five feet two. I was five feet ten. You do the math. I'd go for a little air kissing kind of hug, but not Chava. She pulled my frame down to meet hers for a full frontal assault. My cheek pressed into hers and the smell was just a little like home—a mix of the menthols she pretended she didn't smoke anymore and the distinctive scent of Aqua Net hairspray.

Chava did not go for the unscented kind. She believed everyone should know how hard she worked on styling her hair. She didn't hide the spray, so why hide the scent? It also saved on perfume. Chava apparently got stuck at the age of eighteen back in 1985.

I am not making this up.

This time, however, I only got a faint whiff of the aerosol spray. The hair itself had been bundled up in a long scarf, which wrapped around her head and neck and covered half her face. With her dark sunglasses on, she looked like a starlet hiding from the paparazzi. Chava did not do well in the cold.

Which is why this visit in December made me very, very worried.

Pulling away, I looked down toward eyes that would mirror mine exactly, if I could see them through the opaque, oversized lenses. "Violet," she always said about our eyes, "just like Elizabeth Taylor's."

Our similarities ended there, however, both to each other and to Elizabeth Taylor. I apparently took after the Zapata side of the family. Where Chava was short, soft, and zaftig, I was tall, lean, and angular. Her hair—currently a fine ash blonde— would be a mousy brown shot through with gray if it weren't for L'Oréal. Mine, on the other hand, was black and thick. She piled hers on her head in a 'do I called a bouffant when I wanted to push her buttons. I went with something Chava called a shag when she wanted to push mine.

"Chava. I had no idea you were going to—"

"I know. I know. You're busy. Don't worry. I'll just get the keys to your place and be on my way."

"*My* place? You plan to stay with me?" Usually when Chava visited I put her up in a very nice, reasonable hotel nearby.

Kendra chose just that moment to arrive. A wrap of some unrecognizable dead animal curled around her shoulders. Her makeup was impeccable, and her blonde hair was sun-kissed, thanks to chemicals, and tousled in a way that undoubtedly took hours to achieve. It did not smell of Aqua Net.

"I'm sorry I'm early," Kendra said, taking in my mother's hot pink, velour leisure suit without batting an eye. "Have I come at a bad time?"

"You must be one of Edwina's client's. I'm her mother," Chava said, shaking hands with a perplexed Kendra Hallings. "I'll just wait—"

"Edwina?" Kendra said. "I wondered where the Eddie came from."

"Here, Chava," I said, pulling my house key off the ring. "Can you find my place from here?"

"I'll have to call a cab," my mother continued. "I can wait outside. It's not raining too badly, is it?" She looked around, suddenly helpless. I'd seen the act before, but Kendra fell for it hook, line, and sinker.

"Oh, no, Mrs. Shoes," Kendra said. "You have to wait here, where it's dry."

"Schultz," Chava corrected her.

"What?"

"Schultz, not Shoes."

Kendra looked from my mother to me. "Edwina Schultz?"

"Would you keep a name like that if you had it?" I asked, sliding the house key back on the ring. "My Subaru is parked out back. Take it." I wasn't going to get into a fight over how Chava got to my office to begin with, as she had to have taken a cab from the airport.

"But how will you …." Chava started to make an empty protest about taking my car, but I knew her game. It was how she'd end up looking like she didn't ask for it.

"Don't worry about it. I'll see you later. And don't smoke in my car."

"Edwina! You know I quit."

"Should you have a sudden relapse, please do it outside."

Chava, knowing to stop while she was ahead, exited in a flurry of rolling bags and gear. Had Kendra not arrived when she did, I might have gotten Chava over to the hotel, but now she had both my car and my house, I realized getting rid of her might take an act of God—a being I didn't have on speed dial these days.

"That was your mother?" Kendra asked. I wasn't sure if she was surprised I actually *had* a mother or that my mother looked like Chava Ester Schultz, not Chita Rivera, who, incidentally, I looked a lot more like.

"The one and only."

"You call her Chava?"

"She prefers it that way," I said, not wanting to get into my family history. Chava got pregnant at fifteen and gave birth to her only child not long after getting her first driver's license. She didn't want anyone calling her "Mom" before her twentieth birthday, so Chava it was.

"Here, take a seat," I said, holding my arm out to usher her into a chair and hopefully dissuade further conversation about my mother. The differences in our looks and closeness of our ages always encouraged conversations neither one of us liked to pursue.

That reticence was one of the few things my mother and I had in common.

Before I got started with Kendra, I walked over and closed the door Chava had left open in her haste to get out before I changed my mind. Then I sat down next to my client. Taking a deep breath, I pushed thoughts of Chava Ester Schultz out of my head, hard on the heels of my thoughts about Chance Parker, which were also vying for my attention, and focused on the woman in my office. Swinging my laptop around to face us, I pulled up the slideshow.

"I have some information for you," I said, preparing Kendra for what she was about to see.

"Wait," Kendra said, putting her hand on mine. "There's something I need to tell you before you show me whatever it is you're going to show me."

My heart sank. What now? Whatever complication Kendra planned to throw at me, I didn't want to hear it. I wanted to collect my check and go deal with my mother. I looked at Kendra, hoping her issue would be something simple. But as the pause got longer, I could hear an annoying little voice whisper in my ear, "If wishes were horses, even beggars would ride."

Chapter Five

---•---

I'D BEEN A HIGH SCHOOL dropout. A year after ending my high school career, leaving home was easy. I'd already irreparably damaged the relationship with my closest friend and Chava and I were drifting apart. At eighteen, I left Spokane and spent a few years at loose ends, until moving to Seattle and answering a want ad from a private detective looking for a girl Friday.

Benjamin Cooper was a gem. Perhaps a bit on the rough side, but even a diamond starts out that way. He hired me despite the fact I could barely use Microsoft Word, knew nothing about bookkeeping, and rarely arrived at the office on time. He taught me everything I know about private investigation. The day I got my own PI certification was the proudest day of my life, and maybe the proudest day of his. After he took his own life, I decided I needed to live somewhere that wasn't haunted.

Coop always said, get the retainer paid up front. Always. No matter who the client is, even if it's a friend. Especially if it's a friend. I'd never wavered from that.

Until Kendra Hallings.

For some reason, the woman convinced me to take her on

as a client, promising to pay the retainer in full at the end of our next meeting. She didn't carry cash or a checkbook, she'd explained. And I didn't take credit cards, of which she flashed plenty. She'd smelled like money to me, and I let my guard down, probably because it seemed to be the only way to get her to quit crying at the time.

And yes, I admitted it, I felt sorry for her. Something about her reminded me of that best friend I'd had and lost back in Spokane.

She had big brown eyes and looked as fragile as fine China. I could no more say no to her than club a baby seal to death. I just wanted to pat her on the head and tell her everything would be okay.

"My financial situation has changed a little," she said.

"You look like you're doing okay from here," I said, gesturing at her fur coat.

"My husband has money. I don't."

"You must have your own accounts."

Kendra shook her head; then the tears started again. "My husband controls everything. I either have to ask him for money or go somewhere he has credit. I have a gas card, a few charge cards for clothing, and a grocery card, but not a bank card or access to cash. I don't have a bank account of my own."

I did some quick math in my head, thinking how many times she'd have to fill my gas tank to equal what she owed me. Given the cost of gasoline, not as many times as one might think.

"But something awful happened last night."

My ears perked up at that. Did Kendra already know about Deirdre's death?

"What was that?" I asked, demonstrating my exceptional interviewing skills.

"This morning he took all my cards away and told me he'd have to approve my spending. He said I had gotten too careless with money and I'd have to go to him for everything."

I wasn't sure what that had to do with the affair or the death of Hallings's mistress, but I did have the tingling sensation that told me I was about to get stiffed. I couldn't exactly have the woman go to her husband to ask for money to have him followed.

"How about you pawn something. Maybe this fur?" I said, reaching out to touch her wrap. "What is this, a shawl?"

"It's a stole," she corrected me with surprisingly little condescension. "But it's not real," she said. "Matt's always been frugal and he didn't think anyone could tell the difference anyway, so why spend the money if we didn't have to?"

That might explain the cheapness of last night's hotel.

"You must have something you can give me for compensation," I said, holding out the box of tissues I'd gotten out in anticipation of my visit with Mrs. Hallings, thinking $2.99 a box as I handed it over.

"I don't know," Kendra said, taking out a fistful of Kleenex and blowing her nose in a dainty way. I wondered how she did that. If I cried like she did, I'd have bloodshot, swollen eyeballs and snot running down my face. Honking into the tissues, I'd sound like a burro with a cold, while Mrs. Hallings just looked more and more precious and in need of rescue, like a heroine from some bizarre fairy tale—the princess and the overbearing car salesman.

"Why didn't you tell me this in the first place?" I asked after her sobs subsided enough for me to be heard again.

"I didn't know he'd take my credit cards away. I figured I'd find a way to get the money to pay you. You know, buy something then return it for cash. I had to get documentation about what he's doing."

"So you could confront your husband?" That didn't feel like the safest thing for this lady-in-distress to do. After all, his mistress had ended up stuffed inside the wall of an old building. "You could have followed him yourself for free."

"I don't want to confront him; I want to divorce him. We have a pre-nup that says if I cheat on him, I get nothing, but it also says if he cheats on me, I get half his assets." Kendra's eyes glittered, and this time it wasn't because of the tears.

Maybe the little princess wasn't in as much distress as I thought.

"I think I have good news for you," I said, turning back to the computer. First I'd go through the documentation on the affair, then I'd mention Deirdre's death. I was now very curious about how Kendra would react to that little piece of information.

Maybe there was more to Mrs. Hallings than met the eye.

Chapter Six

―――――・―――――

PUTTING THE FINANCIAL ISSUE ON the back burner, I clicked a few keys and brought up the slideshow of Mr. Hallings and the office manager.

Kendra sat quietly as I clicked through the photos. Once Deirdre appeared in the background of a shot of Mr. Hallings at the dealership, I paused the slideshow. A chill ran through me as I realized the lovely young woman in the photo had died less than twenty-four hours ago, and I might have crossed paths with her killer. Did she die because of the affair? Hallings? Another jealous boyfriend? Or was she just in the wrong place at the wrong time?

Could I have done anything to stop it?

"Do you recognize the people in this picture?" I asked Kendra. There were several women in the photo, and I was curious to see if Kendra had a wife's intuition about Deirdre.

"Let's see ... this is Shelly Woods, she's a sales person," Kendra replied, the PC title rolling off her tongue with practiced ease. "I assume these are customers." She pointed to a small cluster of people standing around a brand new minivan. "That's it. Well, of course that's my husband there," she said clicking her fake nail against her husband's face on the screen.

Deirdre peeked out over his shoulder, and I wondered why Kendra didn't ask about her. She'd referenced everyone in the photo except the beautiful young woman standing too close to her hubby. I turned and looked at her, but all I got back was the wide-eyed innocent gaze I'd begun to think was as fake as her mink stole.

"Moving on," I said, clicking the space bar to start the slideshow again.

We went through a few more photos of hubby in various conversations with people, including Deirdre, but Kendra kept quiet.

Now my intuition kicked in. Something wasn't on the up and up here, and it wasn't the "Fox" in the henhouse. When we got to the photos of the hotel, I paused again.

"Have you ever been here?"

Kendra wrinkled her pert nose. "That's not my kind of place."

She sat quietly as I scrolled through the photos of her husband arriving at the hotel, then leaving again, but gasped when Deirdre emerged from the shadows.

"That's her. That's the woman from the dealership! Is that who's sleeping with my husband?"

I knew the shock was an act. After all, this was what she'd wanted to find, a way to get a good financial settlement from the divorce, though maybe her pride was wounded by his betrayal with a younger, prettier woman.

"Who is she?" Kendra finally asked.

"Deirdre Fox, his office manager. Don't you ever visit your husband at the dealership?"

"No. I never go there. Why would I?"

"I don't know, a lunch date? Bring him something from home?"

"Matt has a lot of flexibility. If we have lunch together during the week we just meet at a restaurant. I never know who's working there unless I'm introduced to them at the Christmas party."

"Doesn't she answer his phone?" I asked. "Maybe you spoke to her?"

"I call his cellphone direct," she said, then sat for a moment, lost in thought. I could practically smell the smoke.

"This is enough to prove infidelity," I said, thinking about the money she owed me. Something about this situation tweaked me and I wanted to be shut of Mrs. Hallings.

"Do you think so?" Kendra asked. "Shouldn't I have photos from inside the hotel room?"

"Your husband can't argue they were there to do paperwork. Not with her dressed like that. But there's something else we have to talk about."

Kendra turned away from the computer screen and looked at me with her puppy dog eyes. I wasn't sure what I expected from Kendra when she learned the mistress was dead. But it certainly wasn't what she actually did—that took me by surprise.

Chapter Seven

———•———

AFTER KENDRA BURST INTO TEARS, I tried desperately to calm her down. As convenient as her crying had been in earlier conversations, this felt genuine to me, tinged with an edge of panic. Was she worried her husband had done the deed? Or was she the culprit and couldn't imagine the body would be found so fast? Her reaction piqued my curiosity about Deirdre's death even more. What was really going on here? I finally got her to stop sobbing, but she didn't want to explain.

She locked herself in my bathroom for several minutes, making me wonder if I'd have to find a creative way to break in and retrieve her. Luckily, she appeared before I had to do damage to my door—makeup fixed and eyes clear. The lady must have stock in mascara and Visine, given the amount of time she spent crying. Saying she would be in touch, she grabbed my box of Kleenex and left.

I mentally added the $2.99 to her bill, but wondered if I'd ever see a dime of what she already owed me. What leverage did I have to get her to pay me? I anticipated she'd be in contact because she'd need my photos to take to a divorce attorney, but what about the situation with Deirdre's death? How did that fit in?

After spinning my computer around to face my side of the desk, I went over to close the door Kendra had left open. Stepping out into the hallway, I could see the outer door hadn't closed all the way. She'd definitely left in a hurry. Walking down to the exterior door, I peeked out onto the street, partly because I wondered what kind of car Kendra drove. I saw her getting into a silver Lexus with a man behind the wheel. It certainly wasn't her husband. First, it was unlikely he'd wait outside while she went in to talk to me about his infidelity, and second, this guy didn't have that great head of hair. I couldn't see his face, but he looked shorter than Hallings; he didn't sit much taller than Kendra. As soon as Kendra got in, he pulled away from the curb, never looking in my direction. I wondered briefly if Hallings wasn't the only one cheating.

None of your business, I said to myself, and returned to my office. Shaking off the day's interruptions, I opened a browser and worked on business for other clients.

The majority of my daily grind consisted of background checks on workers, such as nannies or contractors, and tracking down deadbeat dads, and the occasional deadbeat mom—I didn't worry about those women the way I might for a cheating wife. The ex-husbands hadn't gotten violent during the divorce, so I figured it was safe now and everyone should support their kids. I also worked for attorneys on occasion, finding witnesses or following leads the police either couldn't or wouldn't pursue. I did the bulk of it from right here in my office. The Internet had made it possible for PIs to do a lot of what used to involve footwork sitting in front of a computer screen.

Most of my activities didn't require me to be armed either, but I still owned a gun.

An old Smith and Wesson Colt .45, inherited when Benjamin Cooper died, sat locked in my gun safe. He'd used a different gun to kill himself. Once the police determined his death a suicide, that gun technically belonged to me as well, but I refused to pick it up from where it was held as evidence and asked for it to be destroyed. They'd melted it down. Every once in awhile I wondered what reincarnation that metal went through, and what it was now.

The Colt, however, I'd trained extensively with, and had all the appropriate paperwork to carry as a concealed weapon. The times I carried a weapon were rare. I stayed away from jobs that might get ugly for me. My day-to-day was much less exciting than television would have you believe.

Most of the time.

I worked for a few hours, but my heart wasn't in it. The death of Deirdre Fox distracted me. Though I didn't know the woman, I'd seen her alive the night before. She might have made some bad life choices, but that didn't mean she deserved to die. I wondered which of those choices led to her being stuffed behind a crawlspace in an abandoned building. Had she died by accident and been disposed of when someone panicked? Or through a carefully planned premeditated murder?

Chance Parker had thrown me off even more, almost as much as having my mother show up on my doorstep. It was not a good day for concentration. I shut down my printer, closed up my computer, and got ready to leave. I hadn't heard a peep out of Chava, so I figured it was time to go home and deal with her surprise visit. Maybe she only planned to stay a few days and I could work a few extra hours so we'd keep from killing each other with false kindness. It wasn't that we didn't appreciate spending time together; we just had nothing in common. And we had a tendency to overreact to imagined slights, a dynamic I wasn't sure how to change.

Pulling my office key out of my pocket, I remembered Chava had my car. I knew I could call her to come pick me up, but the prospect gave me the willies. I hadn't asked Chava for a ride since I was a kid. Experience had taught me she wouldn't always show up when she said she would. And nothing felt more like abandonment than waiting on a street corner for a parent who never arrived. Zipping up my coat, I walked past the mailbox, dropped in my letter, and continued on the few more blocks to the bus stop.

Public transportation was never my idea of a good time, but it beat paying for a taxi. As the Red Line bus rattled along State Street, it gave me the opportunity to rub shoulders with the denizens of my community. By the time we reached the stop closest to my house, I'd rubbed enough.

Stepping out on the sidewalk, I noticed the air had turned even colder. The lack of rain made me wonder if we might be in for a snowstorm. Maybe Bellingham would have a white Christmas after all. Not that Christmas mattered much to me. Technically I'm a Jew. Judaism is passed from mother to child, so I qualified in the eyes of the rabbis. Chava never practiced much of anything, so I rarely thought about it, which is why I was confused by the lit Menorah in the window of my home.

"What's with the candelabra?" I asked as I opened the door.

Chava stood near the doorway to the kitchen, wiping flour off her hands onto a spanking new apron that had "Kiss the Cook for Luck" stitched in gold thread on the front.

"That's not a candelabra. That's a Menorah."

"I know what it is. I'm wondering what it's doing in my window."

"I thought it was time we explored our Jewish heritage."

"Now?"

"Why not now?"

I took a deep breath and counted to ten as I walked back to my home office, where I saw the bed made up on the sofa and Chava's clothes hanging in the closet. That's when I realized I had a much larger problem than I originally thought. She had everything unpacked and her suitcases were nowhere to be seen, signaling a stay much longer than a few days.

Turning on my heel, I headed into my bedroom and set my

laptop down on the bed. It had become clear to me my home was no longer my own. Also noticing the stifling heat, I took off a few layers of clothing.

I checked the thermostat. Seventy-eight degrees. I turned it back down to my usual fifty-five only to hear Chava piping up behind me, "We'll freeze at that temperature."

"It's nice and warm in Las Vegas."

"How can you stand it so cold?"

"It's like a hothouse in here! I already feel like an orchid and I just walked in the door. Do you know what my electric bill will be if you keep it at that? Even if it's just for a few days." I ended with hope in my voice despite all the evidence to the contrary.

"We can argue about the heat later," she said, neatly sidestepping my hint about how long she planned to stay. "Right now I've got dinner waiting for you."

"You cooked dinner?"

Chava turned to glare at me, which was impressive despite her short stature. That woman could give me the eye in a way that made me ten years old all over again.

"What?" I said, hands up in a gesture of innocence. "When did you ever cook?" Dinners when I was a kid usually came wrapped in tin foil or from a takeout box.

"I just thought it would be nice for you to have a home-cooked meal after a long day at work." It hadn't really been such a long day, but I didn't need to tell that to Chava. "You could be a little grateful," she continued as she crossed back to the stove.

"Isn't it a little early for dinner?" The clock on the wall read 4:30.

"It's dark already; that's good enough for me. Aren't you hungry?"

"I could eat," I said, my stomach grumbling. After all, I hadn't had lunch.

There was a tiny dining nook in one corner of my kitchen. It faced my equally tiny backyard and the neighbor immediately behind me, who wasn't tiny at all. Luckily we'd both allowed the trees and bushes between our places to run wild, so we couldn't actually see into each other's windows. The growth provided a semblance of privacy. With the early dark of a winter day, however, my current view revealed nothing outside. Just the glass reflecting back the warm glow of the light over the stove and the candles Chava had set out on the table.

I slid onto the bench seat built into the nook's pop out and promised myself I wouldn't lose my temper.

"It smells great. What did you make?"

"Pancakes."

"For dinner?"

"Give me a break; I just started to learn. I haven't gotten past breakfasts."

"I look forward to an omelet in the morning," I said under my breath.

"What's that?"

"Pancakes sound good."

She placed an enormous stack in front of me and in the gloom of the candlelight, I noticed butter and syrup already on the table.

"Don't you think we could have a little more light? You aren't the person I want a romantic meal with."

"Does this mean you have someone new in your life?"

"Don't change the subject. What's with the candles?"

"I just wanted it to be nice."

"It's nice, but I can hardly find my silverware."

I popped up and went over to flick on the overhead light. Chava scurried to wrap the scarf back around her face, but not fast enough to keep me from seeing her black eye, visible in the brighter light despite a layer of makeup.

"What happened to you?"

"I was going to explain it first and then show it to you," she said, dropping her hands.

Bending closer, I could see the purple bruising around her

eye had started to turn yellow. I guessed the damage was at least a week old.

"Who did this?" I asked.

"I don't know," she said, her voice uncharacteristically low. "I got mugged."

"Oh, crap. I'm sorry. Here, sit down." I half pushed, half pulled her over to the other bench and sat her down.

"The pancakes are going to burn," she said, gesturing to the stove.

I went over and flipped the pancakes, standing for a moment to get my bearings. I was used to Chava being able to take care of herself. Seeing her bruised like this made her vulnerable in a way that moved me more than I'd have expected.

"Did they catch him? Them? Whoever did it?"

"Can we talk about it later?"

Something in her voice made me turn from the stove. I looked her over again, and when she ducked away to break eye contact I realized it wasn't because she didn't want me to see the bruises.

"You know who did this to you, don't you?"

"Not exactly—"

"Ah, crap. You weren't mugged. You did it again, didn't you?"

At least she had the decency to look embarrassed.

Chapter Eight

CHAVA HAD ONE VERY SPECIAL talent that made her an exceptional poker player. She could count cards. Casino owners frown on card counters—or "advantage players," as they call them, since it shifts the advantage from the house to the player. A few years ago, I learned Chava had counted cards one too many times at a particular casino, been escorted out by large, intimidating men, and instructed to never darken their doorway again.

"Let me guess: you've been eighty-sixed from another casino and it involved large men whose fists made contact with your eye."

"Not exactly."

"So, what, exactly?"

Chava had a tell I could read a mile away when she wasn't being honest with me. I watched as her tongue tapped against the corner of her mouth, the tip flicking against the skin of her lips like a lizard testing the air.

"Don't lie to me."

"I wasn't exactly eighty-sixed from a casino," she said,

tucking her tongue back inside her mouth, "I was eighty-sixed from Vegas."

"The entire town? You've gotta be kidding me."

"I wish I were."

"So go to Reno."

"I think it extends to the entire state of Nevada."

"The entire state of …." I sank back on the bench seat and stared at the stack of pancakes growing cold on the plate. As I pondered the enormity of the situation, a little voice spoke up in my head, telling me what Chava was really after.

"You aren't just here for a visit, are you?"

"I thought I could stay with you until I figure something else out."

"I don't want to live with you."

"What kind of way is that to treat your mother?"

"The kind of way I learned *from* my mother."

"What's that supposed to mean?"

"You aren't exactly the maternal type. You never really took care of me. Why should I take care of you?"

"That's a terrible thing to say."

"What, the truth?"

"I did the best I could as—"

"Yeah, yeah, yeah, I know. I've heard the line before. Poor you, struggling along, a single mother, a teenager, with a kid to take care of. Did it ever occur to you a child doesn't like to hear what a burden they are on their only parent?"

"You know I never meant it that way."

What other way could she have meant it?

"Why don't you go somewhere else where there's gambling? Laughlin? Atlantic City? New Jersey doesn't allow casino owners to toss card counters; you'd do fine there."

"Would it really be so bad to have me live with you for a little while? You have the room. I won't—"

"What? Be a burden?"

Chava had the decency to blanch at my comment. I guess hearing it about herself wasn't as easy as saying it about me. She did have one thing right, however: I had the room. And she was my mother. I could feel myself beginning to cave.

Chava could feel it too.

"Your pancakes are getting cold. Let's just finish dinner and we can talk about it again in the morning."

My stomach growled. I had to admit the pancakes were pretty tasty, and having food made for me was awfully nice. I poured on a little more syrup and took another bite.

Chava saved the pancakes cooking on the griddle. They were a little brown, but not burnt, so she slathered them with butter, poured syrup, and took a bite.

"I'm sorry about your eye. Did it hurt?"

"You should see the other guys," Chava said as her humor returned.

"I'm being serious. You could really get hurt one day tangling with casino security, more than just a black eye."

Chava shrugged away my concern and changed the subject.

"So, how was your day?"

I rolled my eyes at the cliché conversation starter, but I had to give her credit for trying.

"Not bad. I finished up a few things."

"Tell me about it."

"You wouldn't be interested," I said, unwilling to let go of the righteous indignation I'd built up at Chava crashing my home.

"I'll bet I would. I always wonder exactly what it is you do."

"You hate that I'm a PI."

"I hate the thought you could be in danger. The fact you're a PI just makes me proud."

I looked hard at the corner of her mouth, but her tongue stayed firmly planted behind her teeth. It never occurred to me Chava might worry about my wellbeing.

"I always figured you'd be the best PI around. You were good at everything you did."

"That is *so* not true! I was a total disaster at ballet, piano, roller skating—"

"Yeah, but you never really tried at those. Look how good you were at karate and track and field. Those things mattered to you and you excelled."

Now I had two pieces of information to puzzle over. Chava worried about me and she noticed what I was good at. It was a day for surprises.

I decided to take a chance and tell her about the death of Deirdre Fox.

"So you were taking pictures of her affair with a married man one minute, and the next minute someone is stuffing her lifeless body into a hole in a wall?" Chava said.

"Pretty much," I said, feeling even worse about Deirdre's fate than I had before.

Maybe telling Chava about my case had been a mistake.

I didn't fill her in concerning my past relationship with Chance Parker. I didn't even mention his name. Chava had an uncanny ability to discern exactly how you felt about a person by how you said their name. I wasn't interested in hearing her speculate about my feelings for Chance, especially as I wasn't sure myself.

"Maybe that girl lived up to her name," Chava continued, proving my point about her obsession with appellations. "Her mother never should have named her Deirdre."

"What's wrong with Deirdre?" I asked, eyeing a mother who had named her child Edwina.

"It means 'woman of sorrows.' Who would name her child that?"

"What does Edwina mean?"

"Edwin means 'wealthy friend.' "

"Isn't Eduardo really Edward in English?"

"Would you have wanted me to name you Edwardina?"

She had a point.

"How do you know what Deirdre means?" I asked.

"It's from an old Irish legend."

I sat back in my seat, staring at my mother.

"What? I read," Chava said.

"It's not that. You just asked a very good question. Who would name her child Deirdre?"

I didn't think too much about the meaning of the name. Deirdre's mother probably didn't even know about some old Irish legend. What struck me was I knew nothing about Miss Fox. Perhaps her death had nothing to do with the affair or my client. More importantly, maybe there wasn't something I could have done to prevent it.

Or maybe I could use it to my advantage somehow with Kendra.

"What are you thinking?" Chava asked after I remained quiet for a few moments.

"That I need to do some research into the woman of sorrows."

"Won't that interfere with the police investigation?"

"Not at all," I said with a confidence I didn't quite feel.

What could possibly go wrong?

Chapter Nine

———•———

A**RRIVING AT MY OFFICE THE** next morning, I plugged in my computer and fired up my partner—as that was how I thought about my laptop. Without her, I couldn't do my job. Well, that and a good Internet connection. Deirdre's death had been gnawing at me all night. Had something been going on right in front of my eyes? I had to know what happened and whether or not I should have seen it coming. I didn't think I'd get much out of the police, so I might as well poke around on my own. I started doing a basic background search online about Deirdre Fox.

Because her name was fairly unusual, I didn't think I'd have any trouble tracking down her history. How many Deirdre Foxes could there be?

I found one in Minneapolis, one in Belfast, Ireland, and one D. Fox in Bellingham. D. Fox had no phone number, but I found her address. I decided I'd do a little drive by at Miss Fox's residence and see if she had lived alone.

The streets were quiet, as they often are when even a light snow falls. The Pacific Northwest is hopelessly ill-equipped for wintery weather. A single flurry sends everyone scurrying for home or barricaded inside for the duration. People go into work late. Classes are cancelled. Drivers stay off the roads.

The minimal fluff on the ground would probably only warrant half a day, but folks were going to sleep in and blame the "winter storm of the century."

Deirdre lived in the area where expensive, vintage Fairhaven blended into Western Washington University. With 15,000 students, WWU was one of the six state-funded four-year colleges in Washington. Though not the household name of some of the other, larger schools, it claimed several professional athletes and the majority of the band members of Death Cab for Cutie as alums.

Good enough for me.

Deirdre's side of the hill didn't have the spectacular views of the bay the Fairhaven side had, but there were a few of the grand old Victorian homes left over from the 1800s. Arriving at her address, I discovered one of those old Victorians, divided into apartments. Unlike the lovingly restored showcases facing Bellingham Bay and downtown, Deirdre's Victorian had the rundown air of a rental.

I drove past the address, assured myself all was quiet, then parked and walked back. The property still had the wide front porch and exquisite gingerbread trim from over a hundred years ago, but college students had other priorities than washing windows or painting siding, and no doubt the owners lived out of the area altogether. The winter season had turned the trees and bushes around the property into nothing but bare sticks, and the peeling paint and weathered window frames stood out more than they would in the middle of spring, when flowers would brighten the weathered façade.

A neat row of modern mailboxes had been attached to the wall just to the right of the front door. They looked as out of place as a fauxhawk on an aging beauty queen, but I loved it when mailboxes were easy accessible to the public, and not behind a security door. Even better, they weren't the locking kind, and I could peek in to see what the tenants hadn't picked up yet. I found no mail in the first two. Number three had one of those Value-Pacs of coupons addressed to Deirdre Fox. The fourth was stuffed with mail, at least a few days worth, and the name of the resident was apparently "current occupant."

Funny, I got their mail, too.

With no nameplates on any of the mailboxes, I couldn't try to bluff my way into conversation with the neighbors. I could, I suppose, just say I was a private investigator looking into Deirdre's background—at this point the police had no doubt searched her apartment, so the neighbors would know something bad had happened to the woman.

The front entranceway of the once stately house was now the common area between the individual apartments. The doors to various rooms had become the front doors to each household. As I stood there debating what to do next, a big, rangy, twenty-something guy—I'm guessing he would appropriately be called a "dude"—banged out of one of the interior doors from the back of the house and came through the front door.

"Hey," the dude said, apparently unsurprised to find a strange woman standing on the front steps of his building at 8:00 on a snowy morning. "You going in or out?"

"What?"

"Should. I. Hold. The. Door?" Snarky as his cadence might be, his lopsided grin showed amusement, not irritation.

"Do. You. Live. Here?" I asked, eliciting a chuckle from the big guy.

"Yep. You need something?" I wondered for a moment if he was offering to sell me something illicit, but he hitched his backpack higher up on his shoulder and continued, "I gotta get to school, but if you need a jump start or something I could wake up my roommate."

I realized I'd gotten way too cynical when a nice, young man offered me help and I assumed there was some ulterior and potentially illegal motive to it.

"No. Nothing like that. I was wondering if you know Deirdre Fox."

"Who?"

"The woman who lives in," I pointed to her mailbox, "unit three."

"Oh, yeah, her. Fox, huh, that's good, I didn't know her name."

"What's your name?"

"Greg. What's yours?"

"Eddie."

"Eddie! Whoa. That's cool. I wouldn't have guessed." I wondered for a moment what name he might have guessed. Jan? Marsha? Cindy?

"Nope. Eddie."

"What's going on with her?" the kid asked as he looked at his watch.

"Why?"

"I came home yesterday to find out the police had searched through her apartment and left us a card saying they want to talk."

I assumed the "us" was Greg and his roommate.

"You haven't spoken with the police yet?"

"No. Is she in some kind of trouble?"

"I'm going to let the police fill you in on that," I said, "but can I ask you a few questions?"

"Are you a cop?"

"Private investigator."

"Seriously?"

"Seriously."

"Awesome. I've never met a private investigator before. Sure, we can talk. School probably cancelled our first classes anyway."

Greg dropped his backpack on the floor and sat down on one of two vinyl kitchen chairs abandoned on the porch. He gestured for me to sit in the other.

"Ask away, Eddie, the private investigator."

"You're a student at Western?" I asked.

"Second year."

"What are you studying?"

"I'm undeclared right now," he said, apparently unconcerned I was asking him personal questions.

"Time enough for that later, right?"

"That's how I see it."

"So how long have you lived here?"

"Since August."

"Did Deirdre live here when you moved in?"

"No. I know that apartment was empty because my roommate and I looked at both that one and the one we're in."

"You're in, what? Apartment …."

"Two," he filled in the information for me. "We live downstairs in the back."

"So Deirdre's apartment would be—?"

"Upstairs. Right above us."

The kid was great at filling in the blanks. Just the kind of person I loved to interview.

"Can you hear her? When she's home?" I carefully kept her in the present tense.

"Sometimes. These old places, you know, they're kind of noisy. Not a lot of insulation between the floors. The upstairs has carpet though, so we don't hear her as much as you'd think, plus she has a light tread."

"You've never heard anyone else in the apartment?"

"Nope. Just her."

"Do you remember the last time you heard her?"

He pondered that a moment, then shook his head. "I've been at school a lot the last couple days. We're in finals next week."

"Do you remember the last time you saw her?"

"I remember I saw her on Monday—she usually leaves for work after I go to school—but she must have been going in early because I ran into her in the hall."

"Did you talk to her?"

Greg laughed. "I always try," he said. "She's hot, you know, for someone her age." Her "age" being not quite thirty. I guess when you're not quite twenty, thirty seems old. "Fox," he repeated again, "That's her exactly—a stone cold fox."

"She's not very friendly?"

"She's not rude or anything, but she makes it clear she doesn't want to hang out with us. My roommate always tries to get her to come over, you know, if we have a party, just being neighborly, but I guess we aren't her type."

"What is her type?"

"I'm going to bet someone with more money."

"Why do you say that?"

"She always dresses really nice, you know, like she makes *mucho dinero*. But she lives here. To me that says she wants to project the image that she enjoys a certain lifestyle, when she can't really afford it."

"So she lives alone?"

"Yeah. And like I said, I never see her have anyone over. I always thought maybe she didn't want her boyfriends to see she lives like a college student."

"Boyfriends? You think she has more than one?"

"She goes out a lot at night. I see her leave, you know, dressed up. If she had a serious boyfriend, I think she woulda 'fessed up to where she lives, you know? So I figure she plays the field."

The kid might make a good PI.

"What about your other neighbors?"

"Neighbor. There's only one."

"Male or female?"

"Male. A guy named Kemper, lives downstairs next to us, but he's been out of town for a few weeks. He's a grad student and he's always off in the jungle or on a boat or something. Maybe on a boat in a jungle." The dude laughed, and I joined him, deciding I liked his sense of humor. "I don't know where he went this time. The other apartment upstairs is empty."

I heard a chirping sound and Greg started rooting around

in his backpack. I realized it was his cellphone, playing a pop tune I would no doubt recognize if I was more plugged into the young and hip generation. He fumbled to answer it.

"Dude," he said into the phone, proving me right on that account. "What? Where? Okay. Catcha."

He flipped the phone shut and stood up. "I gotta run."

"Okay. Thanks for your help."

"No prob."

Greg slung the backpack over his shoulder and leapt off the porch. Crossing over to a beat-up Honda that might have been silver at one point, he started it up in a cloud of smoke, making his "Save the Planet" bumper sticker into something more ironic than I think he intended.

As he drove away, I contemplated trying to wake up the roommate, asleep in apartment two, but decided I wasn't likely to learn anything useful from him. Maybe I'd do better trying to track down where Miss Fox had lived before she resided at her current apartment. I could always come back later. Maybe Miss Fox had a stalker from a previous life. She was that kind of pretty. I could see a crazy man refusing to let her go, following her here.

"Maybe Miss Fox dated the wrong man," I said to my faithful automobile. "Perhaps Mr. Hallings was one among many, as young Master Gregory surmises." I liked to talk to my Subaru in a fake English accent. It helped pass the time, and my car never judged.

I decided to head home and check on Chava. Maybe I'd get lucky and hear the police had determined who killed Deirdre Fox, and it would have nothing to do with my client or her husband.

And it would be nothing I could have prevented if I'd been paying a little more attention.

Chapter Ten

———•———

Arriving back at the house, I found Chava in the kitchen.

"Oh good! You're home," she said, showing surprising enthusiasm given it wasn't yet 10:00 in the morning. Chava was not a morning person. "Your note said you wouldn't be home until later."

"I decided to work from here," I said as I plopped myself down at the table. "What are you making now?"

"Baked gruyere and sausage omelet," she said with a pride I hadn't heard in her voice since the card tricks she'd practiced on me when I was a child. I had a flashback to sitting in our living room in Spokane. I was eight or nine at the time. "Prestidigitation," she'd said. "It's all about misdirection. Keep your eyes on my hands, Edwina," she instructed as she made my card rise magically through the deck.

Even when she was learning a new one, I rarely caught her making a mistake.

"That sounds delicious," I said and let her serve me up a heaping plateful. Maybe having Chava in my house wouldn't be so bad. We ate breakfast together in companionable silence, sharing the *Bellingham Herald* I'd brought home. Deirdre Fox's murder was referenced, though neither her name nor picture appeared. Without any personal details to exploit, the paper had opted for a short article about a body being found. Mostly it stated the investigation was ongoing and cautioned about the dangers of illegally pulling copper wiring out of buildings, as it could cause death by electrocution.

I wondered if they hadn't identified Deirdre because her next of kin hadn't been located. The idea that Deirdre had no one to mourn her struck me as rather sad. I looked over at my mother and considered the impact on her, should I die a violent and senseless death.

The pancake makeup covering her bruise had begun to flake off and I could see lines around her eyes I'd never noticed before. The idea of my mother getting old had never hit me. Chava was just … Chava. I'd always assumed she looked her age, but realized she only looked her age *now*. Before, she'd always looked younger. And she was only sixteen years older than me.

"You know what I'd really like to do?" she asked, noticing me watching her.

"What's that?" I asked, feeling generous in spite of myself.

"I'd like to cut your hair."

Maybe not that generous.

"My hair is fine just the way it is."

"Just a little shaping. You have such a pretty face."

Chance might like a new look for me.

Where had that thought come from?

"As long as you don't use any Aqua Net," I said to combat my wandering mind. How bad could one little haircut be?

Twenty minutes later, I had my answer.

"I look like a hedgehog," I groaned as I peered into the hand mirror my mother held out for me.

Perched on a chair in the middle of my living room, I sat

with plastic covering my clothes. Chava had taken a large garbage bag and cut a hole in the top and two holes on the side for my arms. I wore it stuck over my head like a poncho. I thought wearing a garbage bag was bad, but looking in the mirror, I forgot about what she'd stuck me in as I inspected how my hair stuck out.

Chava promised to take off just a few inches, but ample clumps of hair were scattered all around me, making me question what "a few inches" meant to her.

"I barely took any off," she protested, reaching her foot out to push the evidence to the contrary around behind me where I couldn't see it. "And you do not look like a hedgehog."

"I do. And you promised not to use hairspray."

"I did not use hairspray. Gel is a completely different product. I think you look cute."

Twisting around trying to see the back, I started to argue with her again.

"You're going to strain your neck. Here," Chava said as she pulled me up and led me into the bathroom. She pushed me down to sit on the edge of the sink and held the mirror up in front of me so I could see my own reflection.

I'd never seen the back of my neck before. It looked very bare. And pale. And vulnerable.

"What have I done?"

"Buck up, Edwina," Chava said, trying to take the hand mirror away from me. "It's not that bad."

We struggled over the mirror for a while until I finally wrestled it back, away from her. Chava made a noise of disgust and left the room. I took a deep breath and looked in the mirror again.

"I don't know why you're making such a big deal out of this," Chava called out from the living room. "It's not as if you ever paid attention to your hair before. What do you care now?"

She had a point.

I also had to admit, the cut was kind of cute.

"Won't I have to spend a lot of time making it look like this every day?" I said as I came back out and threw myself down on the sofa. I didn't want to give up my temper tantrum quite so easily. It felt too good. I slid down inside the slippery garbage bag, the black plastic folding up around my ears.

"All you have to do is rub some product in your hair and go. It's the easiest cut in the world. The less you wash it the better it will look."

I liked the sound of that.

"But I'll have to maintain it," I said, still convinced there had to be a downside.

"It will do you good to take care of something. If you can manage the haircut, maybe next month you can graduate up to a houseplant and some day actually own a pet."

The ringing of my cellphone spared either of us any further confrontation over my hair. It was my office landlord. There'd been a gas leak and he needed to close the building for a few days to do repairs. I figured I could work in the library or a coffee shop if I needed to get away from Chava, and it wasn't like I had a lot going on. With the heat shut off, I didn't want to be there anyway. I said no problem, and reassured him I didn't need to get anything out before the work started, as I had all my current projects on my laptop at home.

I didn't want to tell my landlord there weren't any current projects, save investigating Deirdre's death. No one was paying me, but that didn't mean I wasn't going to get to the bottom of it.

No sooner had I hung up with my landlord than my cell rang again. The caller came up as "unidentified," so I was surprised to hear Kendra's voice on the line.

"Hey, Eddie, it's me. I'm sorry about the way I left yesterday. I know I should have called back right away, but I've been really busy." She sounded neither sorry nor particularly busy, but beggars can't be choosers.

"That's okay. Do you want to get a copy of the photos today?"

I said, actually wanting to know if she had my money, but being oh so subtle about it.

"Can I come to your office now?" she said, almost answering my question.

"I can meet you anywhere."

"Great. Your office, in an hour?"

"Anywhere else," I said before explaining about the workers currently tearing gas pipes out of my walls or whatever it was they were doing.

"Oh." Kendra sounded oddly disappointed.

"I can meet you somewhere closer to your house if you want. I have my laptop. I can burn you a CD."

"Um ... let me think."

I figured she was trying to decide on a place to meet. I waited for a moment, but she remained silent.

"Really, Kendra, anywhere you want is fine. A coffee shop, a parking lot, it doesn't matter. You bring me cash and I'll bring you the CD."

I do take checks, but she'd have to give me the check up front and I'd have to wait until it cleared to give her the CD. She'd also said she didn't have access to a checking account. Maybe she wanted to buy my groceries on her card as a way to cover the bill and didn't know how to bring it up.

"If you're hesitating about how to pay me, we can work something out," I said. "Is that the problem?"

Kendra started to cry again.

Crap. I didn't deal with the crying well in person. Over the phone it was even worse.

"What's going on, Kendra?"

"It's ..."—sob—"it's ..."—sob—"Matt."

"What's Matt? Did something happen?"

"I have another problem. Besides the ..."—sob—"affair."

Great.

"What's that," I asked, trying to channel my idea of a caring individual. I thought I faked it pretty well.

"I'm pregnant."

How much did I really want to know about this? Was she now also worried about child support? And what did that have to do with paying me?

"Are you sure?" I said, "Maybe there's been a mistake?" No doubt I sounded like a reluctant bridegroom being set up for a shotgun wedding, but I was vaguely horrified at the thought of a child being born into this situation.

"Of course I'm sure," she said, a little harshly, I thought, given the circumstances. I chalked it up to hormones.

"Okay, I'm sorry. I only meant, I wondered if this was new information or you've known for some time," I said, back-peddling from the slip up of vocalizing my honest reaction to her news.

Another pause on Kendra's side of the conversation. Maybe she was looking for a little female solidarity. Perhaps I should recommend counseling.

"I'm scared," Kendra said, her voice going even more little girl.

"I'm sure every woman feels that way when she's faced with having a baby," I said, trying to reassure her.

"No. Not that, I mean of Matt."

"Do you think he'll fight the divorce because of this?" I didn't want to ask if they might be fighting about having or not having an abortion or some other complication I didn't want to know about. Mostly I just wanted to get off this phone call.

"I'm afraid he might hurt me, hurt the baby."

Now she brings up domestic violence? That was a new one. When I first met her she'd said he'd never shown any inclination toward that. Had she been lying then? Or was she lying now?

Not to mention the fact that none of this had anything to do with paying my bill.

And did that mean Matthew Hallings had a temper? Bad enough to kill his mistress in a fit of rage?

"Do you want to get together and talk?" I asked, thinking if we were face to face she might be more likely to pay me.

"Yes. But let's wait until your office is available."

"We can meet somewhere else private if that's what you're worried about."

"I'm sorry, Eddie. I have to go. Call me when your office is free."

With that she hung up the phone.

"What the hell just happened?" I asked my cellphone, but it remained stubbornly silent.

The good news was Kendra appeared to be willing to pay me. The bad news was she apparently could only do so at my office.

I was starting to think I should just give the CD to her and be done with it, a little pro bono work so I didn't get caught up with the latest aspect of this crazy-making situation. I'd bet she'd meet me anywhere if I offered up the CD for free.

But where did that leave me?

I decided I'd call her when my office was usable again and try one last time.

This whole situation was making me a little nuts, but I couldn't quite let it go. What should I do next? I thought through my options and came up with something simple. Maybe there was a way I could find out why Chance had moved to Bellingham, which had been taking up a lot more of my attention than I wanted to admit, and I could gather a little more information on Deirdre's death at the same time.

My best friend worked as support staff in Major Crimes, the unit Chance Parker hired into. This meant she was a civilian, not a police officer. Major Crimes worked on homicides not considered domestic. Bellingham only averaged one or two homicides a year, but the unit also investigated assaults, arson, and other felonies. With five full-time detectives, the unit stayed busy.

I rarely traded on our friendship to get information, but this situation felt like it warranted a phone call and I needed to talk to Izabelle anyway, so I decided to give it a try.

I pulled up her office number on my cell and pressed the little green call symbol.

Izabelle answered the phone, the southern drawl of Alabama still pronounced in her voice even after a decade in Washington State.

"Hey, Iz," I replied.

"Eddie! Whach'yall doin'?" It had taken me a while to learn the difference between the singular "you all" and the plural "all you all."

"You wouldn't believe me if I told you," I said, Iz being one of the few people I'd previously regaled with stories of my mother.

"Try me, sister." I always appreciated that Iz could embrace a too tall, white Jew from Spokane as a soul sister for a short black fireplug from Birmingham.

"Chava's in town."

"No shit, girl? Whooeeee! Do I get to meet the estimable Mama Schultz this trip? You know I want to get a gander at the woman who could produce a daughter like Eddie Shoes."

"Maybe. I'm not sure how long she'll be here. I'll fill you in next week at the dojo." Iz and I sparred together regularly at the local gym.

"Next week? What, you got a broken arm? You are supposed to be there tonight."

"I'm going to have to cancel. Things got a little complicated with Chava's unexpected arrival."

And I wasn't feeling quite myself.

"I hear that. Okay, no sweat. Next week it is." I could hear Iz getting ready to hang up, thinking our call was over.

"I've actually got a question for you though."

"Uh-oh. That sounds like business."

"I hate to put you on the spot, but I'm wondering what you know about the investigation into the death of Deirdre Fox."

A long pause made me wonder if I'd overstepped an invisible line, when I heard Iz's voice drop down low.

"Are you asking me to fill you in because the detectives don't want to?"

Basically, yes, but how else could I phrase it?

"I didn't want to bother them," I said.

"I'm not supposed to talk about a case, even with you," she reminded me.

"I know. I just feel responsible. For Deirdre. I may have been the last person to see her alive."

"Besides whoever killed her, you mean."

I held my breath. Maybe Iz would fill in the silence.

I heard her cover the phone with one hand and exchange a few words with someone else before she came back on the line with me.

"Look, I can't talk right now," she said. "Meet me at two at our favorite spot."

I agreed and hung up, wondering who might have been hanging around Iz's desk to overhear our conversation.

Chapter Eleven

I MET IZ AT OUR favorite sweet shop. Pure Bliss created handmade desserts from fresh, local, organic ingredients—the menu included a vegan carrot cake my friend declared the best thing she'd eaten since she gave up meat and dairy. Though I respected her decision, I would never join her, given my deep, abiding love of bacon and cream. On the dessert front, I developed a new favorite every other week.

Stepping inside, I was instantly surrounded by the heady smells of butter, sugar, and chocolate. Iz had arrived ahead of me and was curled up on the bright pink sofa near the entrance. I always envied her ability to take up such a small space. I take up a huge amount of space, vertical and horizontal. Iz, on the other hand, even with solid muscle packed on her diminutive frame, could pull her legs up beneath her and look like she was half her actual size.

"Don't say a word about the haircut," I said by way of greeting.

"Girl! I've been trying to get you to do that for two years. Don't tell me you don't love it. Did your momma talk you into that?"

"Wielded the scissors herself."

"She's a good woman. That's all I'm gonna say."

"If you two are going to gang up on me, I'm definitely not going to introduce you."

"Someone got up on the wrong side of the bed this morning."

"I know, I'm sorry. Life is having that effect on me. Let me get a coffee. I'll be right back."

Standing in line for a latte, I could see myself reflected in the glass case showcasing today's selected delights. I turned back and forth, trying to get a glimpse of myself from all sides. Running my fingers through my hair, I watched it miraculously spring back into place. I had to admit, it was pretty chic. Turning my head, I caught Iz watching me and stuck my tongue out at her. She laughed and went back to chatting with the cute new busboy we'd decided was half our age and only good for long-distance appreciation and harmless flirtation.

"Okay, so what do you know about Miss Fox?" I asked as I plunked down my double latte and balanced my current favorite ambrosia—Chocolate Salted Carmel Cake—on my knee and settled onto the matching bright pink loveseat. I'd already looked around to make sure no one else sat close enough to overhear our conversation.

"You know I can't talk about an ongoing investigation."

"True, but I can tell you what I already know and you can keep quiet if I'm correct."

Iz shrugged, her mouth full of carrot cake.

"Deirdre Fox was murdered sometime between ten and midnight on Wednesday by a person or persons as yet unknown."

Iz sipped her coffee, which I took to be an affirmative.

I mentioned the address listed in the newspaper as the site where her body was found, stuffed into a crawlspace.

"Do you want a bite of this?" she asked, holding out a forkful of carrot cake. I tempted her with a bite of mine, but she held out against the dairy-filled frosting and chocolate ganache.

"What do you think of the new detective?" I innocently

slipped the question into the conversation about Deirdre.

"Seems like a decent guy," she said before looking up from her cake. Something must have showed on my face, because she narrowed her eyes. "What's that got to do with the price of tea in China?"

I sipped my latte, giving her my guileless look. I didn't want to get into my past with Chance. I tried to channel Kendra by batting my lashes, but I don't think I pulled it off very well.

"Have you got something in your eye?" Iz asked.

"Not anymore," I said, dropping my attempt to look innocent.

"I heard a rumor you two knew each other down in Seattle."

"Apparently not that well. I didn't even know he was moving up here," I said without thinking about it.

"That why you're in such a surly mood?"

Crap. I don't usually let stuff like that slip, but I had been thrown off my game by the recent assault on my hair.

"I can't talk about it."

"Can't or won't?" Iz eyed me with suspicion.

"Can't," I said.

"From that comment I can only assume that not only is the rumor true, but what happened between you guys was a lot more serious than Detective Parker let on." I could hear sympathy in Iz's voice.

"Do you know why he left Seattle?"

Iz shook her head. "We've only met briefly. He's pretty tied up with the homicide."

I sat for a moment running all the reasons Chance might have moved here through my head. Had he met someone else? And she lived up here? Or could it have something to do with me? That would be a stretch. We hadn't seen each other for a long time.

But hope springs eternal, no matter how farfetched.

Iz finally broke the silence and let me off the hook. "Information appears to be a little sketchy about Miss Fox."

"Like that isn't her real name?" I was only guessing, but it made sense considering how little I found about her on the Internet.

"Something tells me you've done a little research on the woman."

I nodded. "Her paper trail is a little thin." My next thought was that she hadn't been ID'd in the paper because the police didn't know her real identity yet. I pondered the possibility of remaining invisible to law enforcement in the technology age. Ms. Fox must have never gotten in trouble before, or worked for the government or in childcare or for the military or any of the myriad of other situations that led to being fingerprinted today.

"Her prints don't show up in any databases," I said. That wouldn't be a big leap in logic.

"You should know the cute busboy has been checking out your new haircut," Iz said to distract me.

"Really?" I turned around to look for him.

"What do you think?" Iz said, catching his attention. "Doesn't this hairstyle look great on Eddie?"

"It does," he said, picking up a few glasses at a recently vacated table. "I almost didn't recognize you."

What did that say about my usual look?

"I still think I look like a hedgehog," I said to Iz as I watched him walk away.

"Maybe. But hedgehogs are awful cute."

She had me there.

"All right. I should get back to work," Iz said, standing up. "I'll see what I can find out."

I didn't ask if she meant about Deirdre's death or Chance's appearance in Bellingham. At this point, I'd be happy to know more about either.

Chapter Twelve

———•———

I RAN A FEW ERRANDS after meeting with Iz, so it was getting dark as I pulled into the driveway at home. I could see the Menorah glowing in the window. My mother's newfound interest in our ethnic history amused me. Maybe I'd get presents from her for Chanukah. I let the light draw me inside.

"I'm home," I called out as I came through the front door. It felt kind of nice to have someone waiting for me.

Passing the thermostat on the wall as I walked back into my room to change clothes, I tweaked the temperature back down to sixty-five. Chava had jacked it up to seventy.

"Did your friend like your new look?" Chava asked as I came into the kitchen wearing my at-home sweats.

"She did," I said as I set my cellphone down on the table. "So did the cute busboy."

"How cute?" Chava said with a salacious smile. She was dressed in another velour leisure suit, though this one was purple.

"He's way too young for me."

"So he's just right for me?"

"Ha, ha." I gestured around the gleaming kitchen. "You've been cleaning."

"I thought I should do something to earn my keep."

She was already cooking and cutting my hair, but who was I to interfere with her domestic urges?

"So, are you going to tell me about your latest case?" she asked, picking up my phone.

"No."

"Oh, come on, Edwina. Tell your mother something."

"Just your basic infidelity and pre-nup."

"His or hers?"

"The infidelity or the pre-nup?"

"Now who's the comedian?" Chava said.

"He cheated on her," I said. "She gets half his assets."

"What's he worth?"

"A fair chunk of change, I think. They seem to live pretty well."

"Looking like you live well and actually living well are two different things."

"The wife believes he's worth a small fortune."

"Wives are often the last to know."

Chava had a point. I was taking Kendra's word for it Hallings was worth a lot of money. He owned the dealership, but car sales weren't what they used to be. And he did have her wearing fake furs. Maybe Kendra's payday wouldn't be what she expected.

"You could be right," I said, wondering if money figured into Deirdre's death somehow.

"Hm-hm," Chava said, pressing a few buttons on my smartphone. "I really need one of these."

"So get one," I replied.

"Wouldn't it be cheaper if you and I were on a plan together?" she asked.

Cheaper for whom?

"That would depend on the plan," I said. "Besides, why

would you want a Bellingham area code?" I still hoped there was an end in sight to her staying with me, despite the benefits of home-cooked meals.

"With cellphones today, no one cares where the area code is. I'd love a model like this one." She continued to push buttons on my phone, making me a little nervous.

"Careful. You don't know what you're doing."

"I do, actually. I went through all the features while you were in the shower."

Yikes! What might Chava have done while figuring out my phone? I'd have to make sure she didn't download any apps that would end up costing me money.

"What happened to your old cell?" After all, she'd had one before.

"Oh, you know how these things go," she said. She pushed another button and I heard a click and a ringing sound. A voice come on just as I snatched the phone back, realizing she had called Kendra's cell number back from the last time she called.

"Kendra?" I asked. "Is that you?"

"Kendra can't come to the phone right now," a man's voice said. Maybe the husband? I'd taken plenty of pictures, but I'd never heard his voice. The voice sounded odd, muffled, like something covered the mouthpiece.

"Whom am I talking to?" I asked in my most professional voice. Something didn't feel right here. Why would someone else answer Kendra's phone?

"Is this Eddie?" the voice said.

"It is, and what might your name be?"

"Eddie, good. Kendra asked me to give you a message. She said to tell you she'd be in touch soon and not to worry."

"I'd rather hear that from Kendra myself. Do you know when's a good time to reach her?"

"She's unavailable right now, but don't worry, she'll call you," the man said before he hung up the phone.

Sitting with the cell in my hand, I started running through

possible scenarios to explain what just happened. If the caller was Hallings, he must have found out what Kendra had done because he knew my name. That might not bode well for Kendra. Was she serious about the whole, "I'm afraid of Matt" thing?

If the voice wasn't Hallings's, someone else had Kendra's phone, and knew about me, which again, might not bode well for Kendra. It was possible there was an innocent explanation. Maybe Kendra left her husband and the man answering was a friend. Maybe Kendra had gone to one of those crazy spas where no contact with the outside world was allowed and she'd left her phone with someone.

Or maybe she was as dead as Deirdre Fox and stuffed into a wall somewhere.

"What's going on in your mind?" Chava asked, as I remained deep in thought.

I told her a little bit about the situation, including my confusion about why some guy was answering Kendra's phone.

"Want to do me a favor?" I asked.

"Sure, what do you need?"

Clicking onto the Internet on my cell, I looked up the number to Hallings's dealership and explained what I wanted. Placing the call, I held the phone up between us and put it on speaker.

"Hallings Chevrolet," a perky young female voice came on the line after I placed the call.

"Yes, is Mr. Hallings available?" Chava said in a voice I didn't recognize. I guess if I had a professional voice it made sense she had one too. This must be what she sounded like sitting at the card tables and working her magic on the unsuspecting house.

"Sure thing. May I tell him who's calling?"

"Trixie Apple," Chava said without missing a beat.

"One moment please, Ms. Apple," the perky voice said.

As their awful hold music came on, I gave my mother a look.

"Trixie Apple? Seriously? Where did you come up with that one?"

"No man could refuse to take a phone call from a name like that. Pure curiosity will get him on the line."

I covered my mouth to keep from laughing as I heard another voice on the phone.

"This is Matt Hallings. What can I do for you?" he said. The voice didn't sound like the one I'd just heard, but I needed a little more time. If the man on Kendra's phone had been deliberately disguising his voice, I might have a harder time telling if it had been Hallings. Besides, maybe he was using *his* business voice too. I motioned to Chava to keep him talking.

"Yes, Mr. Hallings. I'm looking for a new car and a friend said I should call you."

"Excellent. What kind of car are you looking for?"

"Something big and reliable."

"Well, we've got an excellent line of SUVs that should fit the bill. Why don't you come down to the lot and see for yourself."

"That would be great."

"Let me just get some information from you. That will streamline things when you get here."

I could hear a rustle of papers as Hallings prepared to fill out a form on Ms. Trixie Apple. Chava looked at me to find out if I'd heard enough. I nodded.

"Oh, look at the time," Chava said. "I forgot to pick my son up at school. I'll call back. I've got to run."

Chava hung up on Mr. Hallings mid-sentence and started cracking up.

"Forgot to pick your son up from school?" I said. "It's twenty degrees outside. What kind of a mother are you?"

"My fake son is tough," she said, still giggling. "He'd have to be, with a mother like Trixie Apple." Chava regained her composure. "So? Was it him?"

"Nope. That was definitely not the man who answered Kendra's cellphone."

"You can tell that even though the other voice sounded muffled?"

"The cadence was all wrong—how he pronounced things. It wasn't him."

"The plot thickens," Chava said. "What now?"

"I think I'll run over to the Hallings's place, take a look around." I stood up to go change back into warmer clothes.

"Okay. Let me just get my coat."

I wanted to point out it wasn't her coat, it was mine, as she had raided my closet for winter clothes, but that would just distract me from trying to dissuade her from tagging along.

"You're not coming with me."

"Why not? You might need me. Look how much help I was with the phone call? Besides, I could use a night out."

I wasn't sure I liked the sound of that, but it was hard to argue with Chava Ester Schultz.

"Fine. But when I tell you to stay in the car, you stay in the car."

"Whatever you say."

Why did I get the feeling she didn't really mean that?

"I'll be back in two shakes," she said as she hustled out of the kitchen, heading for the back room with a spring in her step.

It was just a simple errand. How much trouble could Chava get us in to?

Chapter Thirteen

CHAVA HAD TRADED IN HER purple leisure suit for a black tailored jacket and a pair of blue jeans. Lugging a handbag that could double as living quarters for a family of five, she'd also swaddled herself in my old down jacket, appropriated from my hall closet. It fit her like a puffy tent.

"Maybe I should buy myself a good winter coat," she said, dropping into the passenger seat with the extra fabric of the garment billowing out around her.

"Maybe you should consider a warmer climate," I said to be helpful.

She tugged her seatbelt on and reached out to the dashboard to crank the heat on high. Chava and I definitely had different internal thermostats.

"I feel like I'm in a convection oven," I said, reaching out to turn the heat back down.

"You don't even know what a convection oven is," she said, turning the knob back up a couple of notches.

"Neither do you," I said, turning the knob back halfway. I could see how things were going to go between us, give and take back and forth until neither one of us was happy.

On the way over to the Hallings's address, I explained the situation to Chava—how the dead woman I'd told her about was the mistress we'd talked about earlier. Instead of sobering her up, the news just piqued her curiosity.

"Well, isn't that interesting," she said, and I saw her lean forward a bit in her seat, eager to get a glimpse of the Hallings's house, embroiled as the residents could be in mayhem, infidelity, and murder.

I'd started to regret bringing her along.

People with new money often flocked to the renowned Chuckanut Drive, where fancy houses lined the bluff five hundred feet above Samish Bay. The rest built McMansions on Lake Whatcom—also the source of drinking water for the City of Bellingham. I tried not think too much about people riding around on boats, or worse yet, skinny dipping, through my tap water.

Though my house and the Hallings's *estate* weren't that far apart geographically, our economic statuses didn't exactly overlap. After driving slightly north, then curving east around the lake, we arrived at the address, a substantial lot covered in trees fronting the lake. A tall, stucco wall, with wrought-iron details and decorative lamps that hid the majority of the grounds from public scrutiny. A red tile roof peeked out, the only hint of the enormous house that lay beyond. I was surprised to see a "For Sale" sign in the yard. Kendra never mentioned they were relocating, and I wondered at her leaving that little detail out of our conversations. It was possible they were downsizing—the house was enormous—but the sale could also point to money problems.

"You will stay here," I said to Chava as I parked down the street.

"Why can't I come with you? I'd love to get a look inside a place like that."

"Which is exactly why I'm not taking you. I can't work and keep an eye on you at the same time."

Chava started to argue, but I took the keys and slammed the door. I didn't want her getting antsy and driving off, leaving me behind.

And no, I wouldn't put it past her.

The gate to the property stood open, which seemed to defeat the purpose of having one in the first place, but I appreciated the easy egress. The house, when it came into view out of the darkness down the long drive, stood two stories tall along the low bank of the lake. The warm, sand-colored stucco of the Italianate home glowed bright in the spots of outdoor lighting artfully hidden in the shrubbery. The red terra cotta roof tiles glinted through the stately Madrona trees surrounding it, the distinctive, peeling red bark a nice contrast against the other evergreens in Hallings's mini forest. Walking up to the front door, I could see a security camera mounted on the wall over the door under the portcullis. Its red eye seemed to glare balefully at me, though I always wondered how often these things were just a front and not actually connected to anything.

I knocked. Rang the bell. Waited. Knocked again. Rang the bell.

The Hallings had a live-in maid, so I expected someone to be home, even if Mr. Hallings was at the dealership and Kendra was in the wind.

After waiting a few more moments, I rang the bell one last time and decided to do a little reconnoitering around the property. I stepped off the porch and wound my way through dense vegetation to peek into the windows of the front room. The rhododendrons were tucked into themselves, buds well hidden until spring—the bushes large enough to be a barrier, but leggy enough that I could push myself through. Looking into the front room, I could see the place was in disarray. The coffee table was strewn with papers, and there were blank spaces on the walls where lighter patches outlined missing art work. A chair was overturned.

Now I really had a dilemma. If something untoward had

taken place in the Hallings's residence, I should probably call the police. I thought about the possibility that Kendra had been telling me the truth about being in danger from the man. Would he hit his wife when she was pregnant even though he'd never been violent before? Maybe the baby wasn't his. Or had Kendra lied to me about him being violent?

I contemplated the likelihood that if I called the police I'd manage to escape talking to Chance Parker in person and decided to do a little more reconnaissance before I did anything rash. Continuing around the side of the house, I hoped once again that the video surveillance was either a fake or there wasn't a security firm monitoring it 24/7. I figured it was most likely a live feed, not a recording, though if a security company called in to the police about an intruder it would solve my problem about whether or not to contact them about the mess inside the house. I decided to let fate dictate my actions.

The farther I got from the front door, the less outdoor lighting I had to contend with. Walking around the side of the house, I discovered the Hallings's home had no outdoor lighting in back at all except for a few low path lights leading down to the water's edge. Hallings's dock did not have a boat tied to it as I'd anticipated. Maybe he'd sold that too.

If the Hallings had a dog, I doubted it would be loose with the front gate open. Other than Kendra's current pregnancy, I knew they didn't have children, so there wouldn't be tiny faces watching me through the windows, fingers primed to call 911 if they saw a stranger wandering around. The houses were far apart and the property was heavily wooded. That meant there was a natural break between their house and the closest neighbor—another huge home built on what looked to be a double lot. Moving farther around the house, I discovered the stucco wall fronting the street didn't actually go around the entire property. The fence ended some twenty feet or so after making a 90-degree turn toward the lake. So much for actual security.

Hallings's house and his neighbor to the right were both tucked into a small bend in the lakefront. Though other houses on the lake were visible from their neighbors across the water, these two homes were less exposed, making it easier for me to venture unnoticed into the backyard. Between the cloak of night and the curtain of trees, I felt sufficiently invisible; besides, it was still cold and I doubted anyone was hanging around outside.

The house sat much closer to the lake than the road, with the backyard strip of land mostly taken up by a patio that extended the length of the house. I crossed the colorful, Venetian tiles, threaded my way through a complicated set of patio furniture, and almost fell into an open fire pit before edging up to look inside the back of the house. A gourmet kitchen opened up in front of me, and a living room spread out on my left, maximizing the views from the downstairs windows, while I assumed the master bedroom took advantage of the additional height upstairs for even better views across the lake. The kitchen looked undisturbed, and I wondered if the mess in the front room had nothing to do with anything nefarious, like a dead mistress, and everything to do with the Hallings moving out.

Walking down the length of the glass door, I found that by standing on one foot and leaning out as far as possible, I could almost catch a glimpse into the dining room on the other side of the kitchen. The house sported an open floor plan and I could see the shadows of furniture in the middle room. Balanced precariously on one leg, gripping the edge of the doorframe, I could see through to the front door.

"Find anything interesting?"

The voice, coming from the darkness of the trees, startled me so badly I lost my balance and tipped over into another large bush.

"Holy crap, Chava, what are you trying to do? Give me a heart attack?" I rolled myself out of the hedge with as much dignity as I could muster under the circumstances, which was fairly little.

"See? Stealthy as a cat. You never even heard me coming."

She had a point, but that didn't exactly make me want to congratulate her.

"You aren't supposed to be sneaking up on me at all." I said. "I thought I told you to stay in the car."

"Your phone's been ringing off the hook. I figured you'd want to know."

Chava handed me my cellphone, which I'd left plugged into the charger. Running my fingers around the dots in the correct order—I had set up a lock on the screen so my mother couldn't poke around on it without my knowledge—I went to the home screen and saw an unfamiliar local number but no voicemails.

"Ringing off the hook? There was only one phone call," I said.

"But it might be important."

Since no one appeared to be home or have called the police, I decided to sit myself down on Mr. Hallings's posh patio furniture and find out who'd called.

"Probably some salesman wanting me to buy insurance I don't need," I said, clicking on the redial button. You could have knocked me over with a feather when I heard a familiar voice answer after the third ring. Definitely not someone I expected to have a chat with.

But, now that I was, perhaps I'd learn something useful. If nothing else, it should be interesting.

Chapter Fourteen

——◆——

"Mr. Hallings." I repeated his name with as much bravado as I could muster considering that I was sitting in the man's backyard. I looked up to see if any lights had come on in the house, with the crazy idea he'd seen me peeking in through his windows and decided to give me a ring.

"Yes?" he said, clearly impatient and wondering why someone called him then left a long moment of dead air after he said his name into the phone. Should I hang up? Or was it more important to find out why he'd called? I decided to play it by ear.

"I believe you've been trying to reach me? My name is Eddie Shoes."

"Eddie Shoes? You're a woman?"

"Is there something I can do for you?" I asked. It wasn't the first time I'd heard that response.

"Maybe," Hallings said. "It's about my wife."

I waited to see if he'd elaborate. Had Kendra told him about me? Maybe she filed for divorce and I'd come up as a witness against him and his pre-nup. Or worse, he wanted to talk to me about the impending child.

"I'm wondering if you know where she is."

That set me back a moment. No scenario I had been spinning out had him asking about her whereabouts.

Unless he had killed her and was establishing an alibi, a faithful husband trying to look concerned.

"What's he saying?" Chava asked, leaning in toward me.

I covered the mouthpiece on the cell and waved her away. The last thing I wanted was for Hallings to hear her and recognize the voice of Trixie Apple. She held her hands up to show she'd understood and backed out of my line of sight.

"I'm not sure why you're asking," I said.

"I saw your number on Kendra's call list," he said, as though that explained everything.

"I think you need to give me a little more information."

After a long pause, I heard a sigh and Hallings took a deep breath. "I'm sorry to bring you into this, but I'm concerned about my wife's well-being, so I'm going to be less … decorous than I might otherwise be."

Decorous? The guy ran a car dealership. Where did he come up with 'decorous'? I had to stop negatively stereotyping people.

"Okay," I said, hoping he'd continue without any more substantial input from me.

"I know about the party."

Party? This conversation had made a turn into left field, and I was having trouble following. I leaned back in the chair and looked over to see what Chava was doing. At just that moment, I saw her open the apparently unlocked back door and walk into the Hallings's house.

At least I hoped it had been unlocked.

Maybe Chava's penchant for prestidigitation extended to lock picks. One person in the family with a set was enough, and I thought I'd cornered that particular market.

Holding my breath, I waited to hear the screech of an alarm bring the police and neighborhood watch down on us with equal weight and vengeance, but nothing happened.

Luckily for me, that extra pause on my end forced Hallings to fill in another blank. Many of my best interrogation tactics were based on luck.

"When I asked Kendra about your number, about who you were, she explained to me she'd hired you as a planner for our anniversary party."

"Party planner, right," I said, trying to picture me planning a party for myself, let alone anyone else.

"I heard Eddie Shoes, so I thought, well you know."

"I know …?"

"I assumed you were a gay man."

A gay man would have a sexier name than Eddie Shoes, I thought to myself. Maybe Eddie Stiletto or something fun. *Ooohhh*, Eddie Stiletto, maybe I should reconsider my name.

"So I know that's why the two of you have been in touch," Hallings continued, pulling me out of my momentary reverie.

I wondered why he hadn't noticed the greeting on my voicemail. The one that said "Eddie Shoes, Private Investigator." That's when I remembered the greeting on my cellphone only repeated my number and asked people to leave a message. Either Hallings didn't see my office number, or Kendra only called my cell from her cell and called my office from a different phone. Or perhaps he didn't think one or two calls to my office mattered enough to check that number out.

"Why is it you think I would know where Kendra is?"

"She disappeared yesterday and I don't know who else to call."

I wasn't going to tell the man I'd spoken with Kendra a few hours ago. Though this might explain why she called from a different phone number. Perhaps she knew her husband was tracking her on her cell.

"The police won't let me file a report for another twenty-four hours," Hallings continued, "because there's no sign of foul play."

"But you think there was?"

"I don't know. This isn't like her. She doesn't just wander off overnight and not tell me about it. I always know her whereabouts."

I thought for a moment about the picture of Hallings starting to evolve in just a short time. He went through his wife's phone records. He claimed to always know where she was, despite the fact she'd visited me more than once without his knowledge. I didn't think this guy was nearly as up on his wife's habits as he thought he was.

"Any chance she's with a friend? A girlfriend?" I added so the man didn't go down the road that led to Kendra having something on the side too. People who cheat are often the most suspicious, believing everyone around them is doing the same thing.

And there was the strange man in the silver Lexus.

"Kendra doesn't have a lot of friends. I'm all she needs."

Except the mysterious man currently answering her cellphone. I wanted to ask Hallings if Kendra had needed him on the evenings he spent with Deirdre Fox, but didn't want to explain how I knew about that.

"I'm still not sure why you're calling me, Mr. Hallings. Most missing adults return home within forty-eight hours. I'm sure Kendra is fine."

"Because your number is the last one she called before she disappeared. The only one she called yesterday. I assumed she called to tell you to cancel the party."

"I see," I said, for lack of a better response.

"Now just isn't a good time for us to have a party," he continued, perhaps thinking I was upset about my loss of income. "We'll get back in touch in the future." I wondered if he was canceling the fake anniversary party because of an impending divorce.

"How do you know the last number she called yesterday, unless you have her phone?"

"Her phone is on my account. I can check outgoing calls online."

Learned something new every day. I'd have to keep that in mind if I ever broke down and got a phone on my account for Chava. Clearly Mr. Hallings knew nothing about the other phone Kendra was using. If she'd called from their home number, he would have looked that up too. Had she called my office from someone else's cell? Maybe after her husband cut off her credit cards, she'd hooked up with the guy in the Lexus and used his phone to call. Things felt like they were happening too fast for me to keep up. Between Chance and my mother appearing in town, I was having trouble focusing on Kendra.

Thinking of my mother, I turned around again to see if I could track her progress through the house and saw a light go on upstairs. I really did need to get her out of there, even if I knew for a fact Hallings was in his office several miles away.

"I'm not sure what to tell you, Mr. Hallings," I said. "Have you called local hospitals? Or checked in about car accidents involving Jane Does?"

"Jane Does? You mean she could be dead and I wouldn't even know it?"

I winced at my tactical error—I certainly didn't sound like a party planner—but the sight of my mother waving at me from the window of an upstairs room distracted me. She'd pulled the curtain back, and at first I thought she was just waving hello, but then I realized her gestures were frantic. She wanted me to join her for a little B & E.

"If I hear from Kendra, I'll be sure to let you know, Mr. Hallings," I said, now desperate to get off the phone.

"Please do. I'm very concerned. I'll be passing your name and number on to the police. So when they're finally willing to take me seriously they have somewhere to start."

I didn't like the sound of that, but what could I do? I certainly wasn't prepared to explain my real relationship with his wife.

"That's fine," I said. "Why don't you call me if you hear from her. Now I'm worried."

"Will do," he said, hanging up the phone.

Sliding the phone into my pocket, I gestured at Chava I was coming inside. I didn't want to join my mother in breaking the law, but I wondered what she'd found that had her so excited.

Maybe it would be worth bending the rules just a little bit.

Chapter Fifteen

———•———

I CREPT THROUGH THE DARKENED lower rooms toward the stairs. Furniture loomed out of the shadows—a large formal dining set, a hutch, or was that a credenza? I could never remember the difference. In the dim light I saw marks in the carpet where other furniture had sat not long ago. Probably a sideboard, given the room I was in. Was Hallings moving his furniture out one piece at a time? Was a sideboard the same as a credenza? Okay, I didn't have time to stop and contemplate why the place felt half emptied or the difference between various forms of dining room furniture. I filed those questions away for later and continued making my way through the house.

The stairs creaked, as stairs do, making my heart jump, even though I knew we were the only people home.

"Chava!" I hissed into the darkness with no response except dead air. "Where are you?" I hissed again after reaching the top of the stairs.

"In here," her muffled voice came back to me. "You've got to see this."

Now upstairs, I walked down the hall toward the sound of

her voice and pushed a door open at the end. It had to be the master bedroom. A king-size bed took up the wall to my right, while picture windows dominated the wall in front of me, overlooking the lake. On the wall to my left were two doors. One stood half open, and warm light spilled onto the off-white carpet.

I always thought people with off-white carpet were very brave. Mine would be white for about ten minutes before it would start an inevitable slide toward muddy brown.

"Come in here," Chava said from behind the closet door, explaining the muted quality of her voice.

I stepped into what turned out to be a walk-in closet roughly the size of my office. Rows of suits, dresses, skirts, coats, and shelves of shoes—more clothes than two people could possibly wear in a year—filled the space.

"So this is how the other half lives."

"There are some very interesting things to be learned in this closet," Chava said, looking pleased with herself. "Tell me what you see, Ms. Detective."

"What I see is you breaking and entering. Tell me what you found and make it fast. We've got to get out of here."

"You sure know how to take the fun out of things." Chava said, but at least she got down to business. "First, didn't you say Kendra told you she wore fake furs, because her husband is so cheap?"

At my nod, Chava turned around and pulled out a floor-length fur coat.

"This is a Marc Kaufman. Genuine mink."

"What's it worth?"

"Around 6K new."

"What about that one?" I pointed at the stole Kendra wore to my office the day when she told me she couldn't pay.

Chava rubbed her hands across it and said, "Fox. Blue."

"You can't tell that by feel. It could be fake," I said, exasperated that she was playing games, when for all I knew Mr. Hallings was on his way home from the dealership.

She yanked the stole off its hanger, found the tag, and pushed it toward me so I could read the words.

"Saga Furs. Not Saga Fake."

"How'd you know that?" I said, my surprise at her accuracy momentarily making me forget my haste to get us out of there.

"I have more talents than just cards," she said.

"Okay, so Kendra lied to me. She wouldn't be the first client to be dishonest about something. Can we get out of here now, please?"

"Not so fast. There's a few other things you should see."

I waited, mentally tapping my foot, while Chava did a Vanna White imitation, gesturing toward luggage stacked above us on a shelf that ran the length of the closet over the area where the furs hung.

"What do you see here?"

"I see ugly brown luggage."

"No. What you see is an expensive Louis Vuitton luggage set."

"How expensive are we talking?"

"A couple thousand," Chava said, getting another grimace out of me. Kendra could have pawned one of the damn things and paid my bill. "Each," she continued after seeing my reaction.

"Okay. I get it. She conned me. Can we leave now?"

"Not quite. See anything else about the luggage?"

I looked back at the bags, neatly placed next to each other, stair-stepping down in size until the last piece, which I think was called a cosmetics case. At least I was more confident about that than I was the whole credenza, hutch, sideboard thing.

"Look closely," Chava intoned, waving her hands around like a bad magician's assistant.

"There's one missing, isn't there?" I said, finally noticing that the stairs of luggage appeared to skip a step.

"Yep."

"Isn't it possible she never had that size? Or lost it?"

"I doubt it. This woman is way too organized. Look at this." Chava pulled out a drawer, showing tidy lines of underwear, rolled into the shape of tubes. The rainbow of colors was laid out from darkest to lightest.

"That's weird," I said. "Who keeps their drawers that neat?"

"It gets weirder," Chava said as she pulled out the next drawer. It was also for underwear—this time black and white, and most important, half empty.

"She packed." I said. "She left on her own."

"Maybe she killed Deirdre Fox," Chava said, "and now she's on the run."

"Or paid someone to do it. Maybe the missing housekeeper was in on it, and now she's on the run too," I finished the thought. "But wouldn't her husband notice her suitcase gone? Her clothes? She must have taken her toiletries out of the bathroom. Why would he lie about it and say nothing was missing? Why would he call the police and report her gone?"

"Did he really?"

"Did he really what?"

"Call the police."

I thought back over our conversation and something twigged at the corner of my mind. "He said something—"

"What?" Chava asked. "He said something what?"

"That didn't ring true. What was it?"

"Relate the conversation to me," she said, excitement building in her voice. Apparently this was more fun for her than a hot streak at the poker table or beating the odds at Blackjack.

I went back over the conversation and got to the part where Hallings said the police wouldn't file a report for another twenty-four hours.

"I can't believe I missed that!" I said after explaining the comment to Chava and actually smacking myself in the forehead. "What a dope I am."

"What? What does that tell you?" she asked. "Isn't that what they would say if there's no sign of foul play?"

"No. People think that from watching too much television. You can file a report any time you want; there's no waiting period, even on an adult. There's just no guarantee the police will *act* on it for a period of time."

"So did she rabbit? Or is he setting up an alibi?"

"And why is the house slowly being emptied of valuables?"

"And what was that sound?" Chava said, anxiety in her voice for the first time since I'd joined her in the house.

Creeping out of the closet, I clicked off the light and stood near the door to the hall.

"That," I said, "was the front door. We've got company."

Chapter Sixteen

———◆———

Tiptoeing to the top of the stairs, I edged my way around the bannister to lean out over empty space and identify who'd arrived on the scene.

A light came on below, momentarily illuminating my face, and I tucked back a step in case whoever turned it on also looked up the stairs. I bumped into Chava, who'd crept up behind me on those catlike, panther paws of hers. At least we both managed not to make any noise. I gave her a gentle shove backward and gestured for her to stay behind me.

For once, she didn't argue.

The thud of footsteps crossing the hardwood floors was followed by deadened thumps on the carpeted section of the dining room. We could track their progress toward the tiles in the kitchen. They sounded heavy, even on the carpet, and I would bet good money the feet making them were attached to Mr. Hallings, not the delicate Kendra, or the missing maid, unless she was built like Attila the Hun. The movement into the kitchen was soon followed by the clinking of glasses, leading me to believe Mr. Hallings was now making himself an after-work cocktail. I fought the compulsion to join him in a dirty martini to hash over the Kendra situation.

"Crap," I said to Chava instead. "He must have been in the car while we were talking. Not at the dealership, miles away."

"Couldn't you tell from the sound of the call?"

"I didn't hear any background noise. He must have been using one of those Bluetooth things. Stupid modern technology."

"Don't deride modern technology ..." Chava started to say, her anxiety at being caught apparently short-lived.

"Now is not the time," I said, cutting her off before she could extol the virtues of my buying her a new cellphone.

I heard more footsteps coming our way.

Grabbing Chava, I pulled her down the hallway toward the rooms we hadn't been into yet. Or at least, I hadn't. Who knew what she had gotten into already? I guessed his next stop would be the master bedroom to change into something more comfortable, and I didn't think his finding us huddled up in his closet would make anyone happy.

Least of all me.

I pushed Chava in front of me down the hall, making for the door farthest from the master bedroom. Stepping quietly into the room, I carefully pulled the door shut far enough to appear closed without activating the actual click of the tumbler. I held my breath as I waited to see if I'd misjudged what room he'd go into. Enough faint light came through the windows behind us for me to see this room had also been emptied. No place to hide if Hallings came in for some reason. I hoped he hadn't heard any noise that would make him investigate.

A moment later I heard the sound of a TV come on from down the hall. I opened the door again and peeked toward the master bedroom. Light seeped under the door onto the carpeted hall, and I could hear the sound of water running.

"What's he doing?" Chava said with her mouth tucked up close to my shoulder. I caught the whiff of a menthol cigarette. That must have kept her occupied for the few minutes it took before she decided to follow me behind the house.

"You were smoking," I said, causing her to back away from me a step.

"Is that really what you want to talk about right now?" Chava said in an urgent whisper, no doubt hoping to distract me from her dirty habit. "We've got to get out of here!"

"Oh, now you're worried?" It was a struggle to keep my voice a whisper when I wanted to throttle her for getting us into this situation to begin with.

"I get it, Edwina. You're a little PO'd right now. But let's focus. What is he doing?"

"I think he's taking a shower."

"So now's a good time to run?"

Without bothering to respond, I edged the door open and moved out into the hall. I could hear Chava's breathing behind me. Her adrenaline was no doubt pumping and her heart racing like mine—though she was also juiced up by the recent nicotine hit. I had the sense that she was more excited than afraid. This was the most fun she'd had since she left Vegas. She wasn't the one who could lose her PI license. I didn't want to remind her that Deirdre had been killed, Kendra was AWOL, and our little adventure might upset the individual who had made those things happen.

Slinking past the master bedroom, I could see that the door to the bathroom stood open without being able to see inside. Chava and I raced down the stairs together toward the front door. I hoped we weren't facing any nasty surprises, such as the door required a key to open from the inside. I was relieved to discover the security chain hung loose and the only thing between us and freedom was a bolt I could unlock with the twist of a wrist and a locking door handle I could reengage behind us. Hallings might notice the deadbolt wasn't locked, but I hoped he'd chalk it up to forgetting to turn it himself. Maybe he'd have a few more cocktails before he turned in for the night and wouldn't remember tomorrow morning whether he did or didn't fully lock the door.

I paused to listen one more time for the sound of anyone coming down the stairs; I didn't want to be seen running across the front driveway if I could help it. Chava got around me and had her hand stretched out to reach for the door handle when I noticed the light on the alarm panel.

"Stop!" I said, trying to balance urgency with volume. Even though I assumed Hallings was still in the shower, I didn't want to take any chances.

"What?" Chava said. "Now's our chance."

"The alarm has been set." I pointed. "Look."

Chava looked at the panel where a bright green glow lit up the "armed" button. "Shit," she said. "Now what?"

At just that moment I heard the sound of the water being turned off. Couldn't the man take a longer shower? He'd barely had time to get the road dust off. Even if we had the time to escape before he could get downstairs, I still didn't know if his security system included video. I didn't want to signal he'd had an intruder and give him reason to watch the tape.

"Now, we hide," I said grabbing Chava's hand and heading to the left. It seemed most likely Hallings would go back down to the kitchen to make something to eat, so any other room felt safer than that direction. I moved through the open floor plan, toward a door on the far wall. Opening it, I shoved Chava inside and followed after her, stumbling down into the sunken room before turning to pull the door almost all the way closed behind us. The faint light from outside illuminated the room enough to make out that all the furniture appeared to be in place: a desk, computer, and shelves of books, leading me to believe we'd come into a home office he hadn't disassembled yet like he had the rest of the house.

"Think he'll come in here?" Chava said. "Should we find something to defend ourselves with?"

"Let's hope he's done working for the day. Now hush, I want to try to hear what he's doing." I leaned against the crack in the door and listened for movement. After a few long moments of silence, I heard footsteps again. The carpeted stairs had deadened the sound of his feet, and I hadn't heard the creak, but I did hear his first step on the ground floor. I tracked his movement back into the kitchen, followed by the sound of the refrigerator door opening.

Turning around, I started to tell Chava we were safe for the moment when I heard a click. She had turned on a green shaded banker's lamp sitting atop a file cabinet.

"What the hell are you doing now?" I pulled the door completely closed to keep the light from showing through.

"Looking in his files," Chava said as if we had all the time in the world to riffle through the man's drawers.

"Stop that! And turn that light off."

"Isn't he in the kitchen? How could he see in here from there?"

"He is for now, but what if he comes this way?"

"Then stand guard."

Arguing with her was clearly harder than letting her do what she was already doing. I still needed to figure out how to get us out without tripping the alarm, so I stood at the door to take a moment to think.

From the sound of pots and pans banging against each other, followed by chopping, Hallings had started to cook dinner. I figured we had at least an hour before we had to worry about him coming into this room. Hearing a click, ping, whirring sound, I turned around again to find Chava sitting at his computer.

"Now what?" I said crossing over to her.

"I thought I'd take a look at his financials."

"His financials? Who are you, Nancy Drew?"

"It's always about money, right?"

"What's always about money?"

"Missing wives, disappearing valuables, dead mistresses. Maybe Hallings is a degenerate gambler and someone kidnapped his wife to get him to pay back what he owes."

"And meanwhile let her pack up whatever she wanted to bring along with her?"

"Just because there wasn't a sign of a struggle doesn't mean a struggle didn't happen. What if Hallings cleaned up the mess and Kendra really did fight off her kidnapper? Or ..." Chava paused for dramatic effect, "Hallings killed her and loaded her up in a suitcase, which he disposed of, so he could later say she ran off."

There was a visual I didn't need planted in my brain.

"Just be quick about it," I said. "I'm going to try to see if I can find sensors in the windows. Maybe we'll get lucky and the alarm is only triggered by the doors."

Scooting over to the windows, I pulled a penlight out of my pocket and started going over the frame inch by inch. It didn't take me long to find a wire clearly attached to a sensor guaranteed to start the alarm screeching the moment I cracked one open. I wasn't even sure the window would open far enough for us to climb out, and on top of that, we'd have to deal with the screen and the shrubbery. Maybe we should just bolt out the front door—the alarm be damned. If we waited until Hallings fell asleep, we would be long gone before he got out of bed to chase us. I'd just have to hope the camera was live feed only.

Chava bent close to the computer screen, reading intently.

"What did you find?" I asked, moving over to stand behind her.

"That it sucks not having my reading glasses with me."

"We are in a bit of a bind here," I said, "thanks to you, in case you've forgotten. You could take this a little more seriously. Breaking and entering is a felony, by the way. I could lose my license."

"Not if we don't steal anything; then it's just trespassing."

"You are not a lawyer. You don't know—"

"Hallings is broke," Chava said, cutting off my indignation.

"What?"

"Hallings is broke. I've gotten into his bank records. He's overdrawn. His credit cards are maxed out. He's broke. The missing furniture? All returned to the stores where they were purchased."

"I wonder where his money is going?" I mused out loud.

"His credit cards also show him visiting the Samish Valley Casino," Chava said, "but the charges are just for food and drinks."

"What does that tell you?" I asked, knowing virtually nothing about the gambling world.

"He's probably gambling with cash," my mother said. "He might have been in private poker games." There was lust in her voice. "It would be enlightening to know if any heavy hitters are in town."

"You could find that out?" I asked, though I could already guess the answer.

"I could make a few calls."

"Well, that could be interesting," I said, not quite wanting Chava to know I needed her help.

And apparently it was going to get even more interesting, because just as I said that, I heard footsteps coming our way.

Chapter Seventeen

———•———

I SHOVED CHAVA UNDER THE desk and clicked madly at the computer, trying to put it back to sleep. Just as I finished doing that, I realized the obvious. Despite Chava's small frame, there was no room for me under the desk with her. Frantically searching for a hiding place, I noticed a small closet door I'd missed earlier in the dim light. Clicking off the Banker's lamp my mother had turned on, I shot over to the door and prayed there would be space for me. If the door hid only shelves, I was screwed.

I tucked into the coat closet just in time to hear the door to the office open and see the overhead light come on through the gap between the closet door and the floor. I held my breath and worked hard at not moving a muscle. The last thing I wanted to do was jingle the coat hangers together. Only two coats hung in the closet, and the rest of the metal hangers sat empty, daring me to breath hard and start them up like a set of wind chimes.

After steadying my breathing, I waited for the sound of Hallings discovering Chava Ester Schultz hiding under his desk. Part of me anticipated what kind of ridiculous story she might come up with to explain her presence. I heard a few unexplainable thumps, then the sound of Hallings's voice.

He sounded remarkably calm for someone discovering a short, middle-aged Jewish woman hiding under the desk in his home office.

It took me a moment to realize what I heard was the sound of him talking on the phone. He must have come in and picked up the receiver without walking around his desk. Hopefully, he would remain that way and not need to get a pen or piece of paper out of a drawer. I listened carefully to his side of the conversation, ignoring the fact my feet and legs were cramping from being in a crouched position under the hangers.

Best guess was a discussion with a realtor. Apparently Mr. Hallings wasn't getting the slew of offers he expected on his palace. He got rather sharp with the other person on the phone, demanding that she—I'd heard the name Joyce—find him a buyer at his current listing price.

"I am not dropping the price," he finally said after a few more minutes of arguing. "Find me a buyer."

With that, I heard the phone slam down in its cradle. I held my breath again. I didn't see any reason for him to open the closet for one of the coats—he must have had one on when he came in—but now might be the time he sat down at his desk and found his legs didn't fit underneath.

Instead I heard his voice again, this time on a much different kind of call. He sounded subservient, maybe even scared. He begged for "more time" and told whomever he spoke to he would come up with the money soon. Then I heard a lot of "uh-huhs" and the phone being slammed down again, followed by clicking sounds I couldn't place.

I held my breath. I wasn't sure how much longer Chava could keep quiet under the desk. A sneeze or a shift in her position would be enough to alert him of her presence.

Then I heard a chirping sound.

"Kendra?" Hallings voice spoke again, and I realized the

chirping sound had been his cellphone. Had the missing Kendra called her husband?

"Who is this?" he barked. Clearly it wasn't Kendra on the line, but was the call coming from Kendra's phone? Why else would Hallings think it was her?

I leaned against the door, trying to hear as much as I could. I guessed Hallings had stood up from his desk and paced away toward the window, because his voice had gotten harder to understand. There was mumbling for a while, then he must have turned back because his voice became clearer again.

"Why should I believe you?" was followed by another long moment of silence as Hallings listened. "Wait a minute. I've got to get rid of someone. Let me call you back from my office; it's more private."

Rid of someone? Did he mean the two women hiding in his house? And wasn't he already in his office?

Instead I heard more clicking and beeping sounds followed by Hallings's voice back on the phone again.

"Okay, now I can talk," he said. "Tell me that again."

There was a long moment of silence, then, Hallings said a few more things I couldn't catch. Maybe Chava was hearing more from her hidey-hole under the desk.

"Fine," Hallings said, his voice clearer. A moment later, I heard the phone hung up and other clicking sounds. The light went out, and the office door opened and closed. I waited another moment, but he seemed to be gone.

I slowly opened the door and crawled out, willing the circulation to return to my legs. Then I cruised behind the desk. I could see Chava's grin even in the shadows, her teeth like a beacon in the dark.

"That was more exciting than trying to fill an inside straight with big money on the table," she said. *Great*, Chava's next career—burglary.

Excuse me, *trespassing*.

"I think we need to wait for him to go to sleep, then make a run for it, even if it means setting off the alarm," I said, pulling her out from under the desk and shifting my weight back and forth to rid my feet of pins and needles.

The sound of a car engine starting up broke through the silence. I crawled over to the window and peered out, seeing a shiny new Escalade pulling out of the driveway with Hallings behind the wheel.

I waited until he'd navigated the long driveway and turned left onto the street in front before I started breathing again and grabbed Chava's hand to pull her toward the door. We'd still set off the alarm, but we would make it out of there long before anyone showed up. Even if the video surveillance did record me on the front porch, I hadn't seen any other cameras, and it wouldn't prove I'd been the one to break in. I could explain I'd come by looking for Kendra. Thanks to the winter weather, Chava and I both wore gloves.

Standing by the front door, I looked at the alarm panel and saw it wasn't set.

"We can go out now," Chava said, starting to reach for the door handle.

"Not so fast," I said, catching her hand. "Out the back. We know for sure there's a camera over the front porch. Maybe there isn't one the other way. We're going out just like we came in."

A moment later found us dodging through the kitchen, where Hallings's dinner sat half finished on the counter. He'd clearly left in a hurry, neither finishing the meal nor putting anything away. On a whim I picked up the phone on the kitchen counter and listened for a dial tone. Setting the handset back down, I gestured to my partner in crime and we went out the back door.

Scurrying around the corner of the house, I walked as far from the front entrance as I could—I didn't want to be picked up in the corner of any video—and we made our way back to my car without further mishap. I breathed a huge sigh of relief as I started up the Subaru and drove away the same direction as Hallings. I didn't anticipate catching up with him, but it couldn't hurt to try.

"Why'd you pick up the phone?" Chava asked.

"I couldn't figure out why he came in the office to make those calls. Then I realized he might have a different business number. I wanted to check the home line."

"And?"

"No dial tone. He's already shut it off."

"What do you make of him being broke? Does it have anything to do with Kendra's disappearance? Or Deirdre's death?"

"You ask good questions," I said. "Too bad I don't have any good answers."

Yet, I thought, *give me time.*

The situation had definitely piqued my curiosity. I wanted to find out where Kendra disappeared to, and whether or not she'd gone under her own steam or with a little help from a "friend." Was she in danger from the same person who killed Deirdre? Or was she in cahoots with them?

"Why would a guy with an elaborate alarm system not turn it on when he leaves home?" Chava asked.

"Because he's not worried about theft," I said. "He's worried about someone coming after him."

"Who?"

"Another good question."

"We're going to find out though, right?"

For the moment, I ignored the "we."

"Could you hear much of his conversation on the cellphone?"

"The call he thought came from Kendra?"

I nodded as we arrived at a four-way stop and I debated which direction Hallings might have gone.

"Not much. It was hard to hear under that desk." Chava thought a moment. "I did hear him say, 'why would you help me,' but I don't know what that was in reference to."

Help him what? Find Kendra? Sell the house? Or something we didn't know about yet?

A few miles later I determined I was never going to catch up with Hallings and decided Chava and I should just go home. Maybe I could find out more about him and his current situation the new, old-fashioned way—in cyberspace.

Chapter Eighteen

---·---

GIVEN THE CONDITIONS AT THE Hallings's house and the disastrous state of Matthew's financials, I could guess Chava had been right and Kendra wasn't going to get the settlement she'd dreamed of. Still, I was curious what had happened to dethrone the King of Chevrolet.

My research showed Chava had been right about Hallings's habits. He was a gambler, and not a very good one. This followed a few years of economic decline that had his dealership selling a lot fewer vehicles than it used to. I traced him to several different online poker games. Apparently, the worse his business did, the more he gambled. The more he gambled, the more he lost.

While I did the Internet search on Hallings, I could hear Chava on the phone in the other room. Much as I wanted to listen in, I decided to respect her privacy. Besides, she'd hear me pick up the receiver and I didn't want to interrupt in case she really could find out something useful.

Not long after I heard her go quiet, she knocked on my bedroom door.

"I think I know what Hallings's problem is," she said, peeking around the door.

"He's a gambler, and not a very good one," I said.

"True, but that's not the real issue. I think his problem is less about owing money and more about who he owes that money to."

"What did you find out?"

"Vincent Careno."

"Who's that?"

"Vegas Mafia."

"Friend of yours?"

"I've played with him," Chava said without rising to the bait. "He's quite the card shark. I hear the family uses him to launder money. He plays very private poker parties with dirty cash, wins big, and turns the dirty cash into clean cash."

"What happens if he loses?"

"His percentages are good enough that it's still worth it. Besides, that's not all he does. He's also been known to loan money to players if they need it for a stake—for a bit of interest, of course."

"Of course. And what happens if people don't pay the loan back?"

"Bad things happen."

"And you think this Careno was playing with Hallings?"

"He came into town and set up a game at the casino. The same one Hallings visited for the last three Wednesdays in a row."

"So maybe if Kendra is missing, she got picked up by the Mob?"

"It's possible."

"I wouldn't even know where to start looking into that," I said, thinking out loud. "Gangsters are not in my wheelhouse."

"Maybe I can get a little more info," Chava said. "Let me make another phone call."

Of course she could. I didn't want to think too much about

whom she was calling. I stepped to the door to listen, but all I heard was the name Rudy. After that her voice dropped too low.

A few minutes later she came back in with a worried look on her face.

"Bad news?" I asked.

"I have good news and I have bad news."

"Give me the bad news first."

"Hallings does owe Careno. A lot."

"What's a lot?"

"Half a million dollars."

"No wonder he's selling everything he owns."

"That's the least of his problems. On top of what he owes, there's compounded interest spinning out of control."

"What's the good news?"

"I don't think they grabbed Kendra. If she's with them, it's by choice. Careno is still in the area. He's staying at the Samish River Casino—the same place the poker games were held."

"Why do you think that means they didn't grab Kendra?"

"Because if Careno was holding on to her, they'd be staying somewhere less public, like a rental house. They wouldn't be keeping her tied up in the casino."

"Does that mean Kendra could be dead?"

"Careno isn't that kind of muscle. He's skilled with cards, but he's not a killer. And he wouldn't have his bodyguard do it either; he's strictly for Careno's protection, Careno carries a lot of cash. No, if the family Careno works for wanted Kendra kidnapped, they would have someone else do it, and there's just no sign of that. None of their known associates have left Vegas for our area."

"Could they have missed someone?"

"If they have, he's very good."

I was dying to know how Chava knew all this. "Just who did you call for this information?"

"I can't talk about it."

"But it's good info?"

"Let's just say my source is very reliable."

I figured Chava either had a friend in law enforcement or in the Mob itself. Either way, I'd have to trust her judgment.

"I always think better with my cards," Chava said, sitting down next to me on the bed and pulling a deck out of her pocket. She dealt them with a practiced hand, not needing to look at what she was doing. We sat cross-legged, facing each other. Chava had decided I should learn to play Omaha hold 'em, since I'd gotten pretty good at the Texas rules.

"Do you think Kendra knew all this?" Chava asked, "about Hallings being in financial trouble?"

"She must have known something. The 'For Sale' sign out front of her house would have given her a clue."

"But why would she still care about a pre-nup that was worthless?"

"Maybe she didn't know how bad the situation was. Her husband could have given her a lot of reasons for selling the house that weren't about being broke. Downsizing, closer to work …" I let my words trail off. Maybe the baby wasn't such a secret and Hallings wanted a more child-friendly house. Something without a giant lake in the backyard tempting a toddler to toddle in.

"How long has the house been on the market?" she asked, tossing the last of the communal cards into the middle.

Setting my hand down, I turned my back on Chava and picked up my laptop again. Looking up the address on the MLS listing service, I located the name of the agent handling the property, the price, and how long it had been on the market.

The house had been on the market for one week.

"Two weeks after Careno showed up in town," Chava said. "Maybe he got into hot water the first night he played with him."

"Can you really lose so much money that fast?" I asked, letting my naiveté hang out.

"Sure. Then he probably tried to fix it the next two weeks and just kept getting in deeper."

"Did you peek at my cards?"

"Are you implying your mother would cheat?"

"I'm implying you would take any advantage a situation might warrant."

We stared each other down for a moment before she finally shrugged and picked up the deck. "No matter what I say you won't believe me, so I might as well deal over," she said.

"That last conversation with Kendra was strange," I said as Chava dealt the cards with her usual practiced flick of the wrist.

"Strange how?"

"It was as if meeting at my office was more important than actually getting the CD with the photos."

"What does that mean?"

I shrugged, trying to concentrate on my cards for the time being, but another thought popped into my head—an image of Kendra pregnant. Was she really trying to make a life for her child?

"Are you going to the police with what you know?" Chava asked, interrupting my visions of Kendra attempting to change her life.

"I don't actually know anything yet. Hallings might owe this Careno money, but I don't have proof of that unless you're willing to tell me where the info came from."

I waited, but got only a negative shake of the head.

"Kendra might be in trouble," I continued, "but I don't have proof of that either. Hallings probably lied to me about contacting the police to report Kendra missing, but even if he did, that's not illegal. He's not required to report anything to the police if his wife left him, and he certainly didn't have to tell me the truth. All I've got right now are a lot of bits and pieces of information and nothing concrete. And I don't know what to think about the pregnancy thing."

"What pregnancy thing?"

I explained to Chava about Kendra's tearful admission she was with child and her fears about Hallings.

"You have to do something," Chava said. I knew she was serious because she dropped her cards far enough down in her lap that I could see them.

"Why?"

"That poor woman!"

"Poor woman? You mean the one who lied to me about her fake furs, stiffed me on my bill, and may or may not be behind her own disappearance?"

"Think about the baby."

"There's no baby. There's just a fetus."

"Not to Kendra."

I looked at my mother, surprised at her vehemence. "You don't know how Kendra feels," I said.

"Maybe not. But I know what it feels like to be pregnant. She said she was worried about Hallings hurting her baby, so she obviously wants to keep it safe. We have to help her."

"Unless she's lying about his violent tendencies," I said. "Maybe she's the one who killed Deirdre in a fit of hormonal rage."

"I don't believe that," Chava said with conviction.

"You don't even know the woman, and what you do know isn't good. You're the one who figured out she'd lied about the furs."

"Things are different now."

"Why does her pregnancy change anything?"

"I don't know … solidarity, I guess. And children have a huge impact on a woman. Kendra deserves the chance to turn her life around."

Given that logic, I wondered how my card-shark, eighty-sixed from Vegas, Mafia-befriending mother would have turned out if she hadn't had me.

"Fine," I said. "I'll see what I can find out about it all. Tomorrow. It's too late to do anything now. Deal another hand."

"There is one avenue of investigation we haven't taken yet."

Avenue of investigation? We? I wasn't sure which comment made me more nervous.

"What's that?" I asked, picking up my cards again.

"The casino. Maybe we can find out a little more about what Careno is doing, or if Kendra is involved with him somehow."

"You mean *I* could find out a little more about what Careno is doing. There's no *we* in this investigation."

"Right, Edwina, because you're not going to stick out at a casino like a sore thumb. That's my territory, not yours. Face it; you need me."

She had a point.

"Can I get you to stop calling me Edwina?" I countered.

"Done."

At least I'd get something out of a potentially disastrous expedition.

Chapter Nineteen

———•———

THE NEXT MORNING CHAVA AND I woke early. We'd stayed up late playing cards, but I think we were both keyed up about finding Kendra.

"Are we out of coffee?" I asked as I looked at the empty bag sitting on the counter.

"Are there any beans in the bag?"

"No."

"Then we're out of coffee."

"Why didn't you say something when you finished the bag?"

"How do you know it was me?"

I gritted my teeth. "Because if I finished the bag I would have known yesterday we were out of coffee beans and I would have gone and got some at the store." I looked over at Chava, who sat at the breakfast nook in an old bathrobe no doubt borrowed from a Vegas Hotel and a pair of blue, fuzzy, bedroom slippers.

"You should always keep an extra bag in the freezer. That way we wouldn't run out."

There was that pesky "we" again.

"I'm going to go get a latte," I said, thinking a quick run to my favorite coffee shop might make the morning seem a little less annoying.

"I'll go with you. Let me just change clothes."

Chava scurried out for the back room before I could say I was thinking more along the lines of going solo, but she looked so happy about the idea I couldn't face her disappointment if I skipped out without her.

We got in the car and headed toward Fairhaven and the Rustic Coffee Bar. We passed other coffee shops along the way, but the Rustic was my favorite. I found a spot right out front, and the two of us made our way inside. I walked in without a care in the world before I saw something that made my heart skip a beat. Standing at the counter was Chance Parker and his partner Kate Jarek. I stopped so quick Chava bumped into me from behind.

"What's the hold up?" she asked, stepping around me and walking farther into the room. I couldn't think of a single good reason to stop her from advancing to the counter, so I edged up behind her, looking at the back of Chance's neck. Maybe he wouldn't notice me.

"Hello, Eddie," Chance said, turning around as if I'd said his name out loud. The look on his face reminded me of our good years together. That brightening up of his eyes when we saw each other after an absence—it felt like he was running toward me as fast as he could go.

I think I said good morning, but I'm not one hundred percent sure it was in English.

Then the look was gone and professional Chance dropped back into place.

Emotions tumbled around in my chest. Seeing him sent shockwaves down to my toes. First, there was the purely visceral physical response I always had to the man, though I wasn't sure why. Not handsome in a Hollywood way, there was still something about him I found irresistible. Start with his height—I always preferred men I could look up to. He was broad shouldered, but not a body builder type, more of a lean, I-can-run-for-twenty-miles-if-I-have-to kind of type. A dash of freckles was sprinkled across his nose like they'd been dusted on with a saltshaker. One ear sat lower than the other. I think I liked that flaw about him best.

"Chava," my mother said, holding out her hand, neatly filling the gap I'd left in the conversation.

"You're Eddie's mother," Chance said, taking her hand. "Nice to meet you. Eddie's told me a lot about you."

I struggled to find my voice. "Chava, this is Chance Parker. He's a local homicide detective." I wondered what Chava could tell about my feelings toward the man, though I think I'd telegraphed to everyone in the room I was in some kind of turmoil. I introduced Chava to Kate as well, and the four of us stood for a moment in awkward silence.

"How's the case going?" I directed my question to Kate, still struggling to put a coherent sentence together.

"Not much to report yet," she said as the barista called out Chance's name.

"That's us," he said with a smile to my mother and a quick glance toward me. "See you, Eddie."

Kate nodded a goodbye as well and the two picked up their cups and headed out the door.

"Hey, Eddie." Chance stopped at the door, looking back at me with a slight smile on his face.

"Yes?"

"I like the hair."

My hand leapt to my bare neck as he slipped out the door.

"So what's good?" Chava asked, and I realized I'd remained standing, frozen, watching the door long after they'd left.

"Rustic Mocha," I said, my words sounding strangled. I cleared my throat and started again. "It's got coconut." My voice came out a little bit stronger.

"Two?" she asked, getting out her wallet. "This one's on me."

Sometimes my mother was all right.

We sat at the counter in the window and I looked out across the street, Chava quiet beside me. We had a lot of secrets from each other. I wasn't sure if that was good or bad. I kept things from her, in part, because we didn't see each other often, and some things weren't meant to be divulged over the phone or through email. But it was also because I didn't want to share. Not about Chance or Coop, the two people who'd mattered most to me since I left home. I'd never told Chava about my dead partner Coop. I told myself this was because I didn't want her feelings hurt that I had needed a parental relationship, but that was mostly crap.

I hadn't told her about him because it hurt too much. I wasn't protecting Chava; I was protecting myself.

"Nice your friend noticed," Chava said.

"What?"

"Chance. Noticing your hair."

"Well, he is a detective. He notices things."

We sat and sipped our coffees for a while.

Chava finally broke the silence. "Do you want to tell me what just happened?"

Did I want to tell her? I wasn't sure.

"You were right," she continued when I didn't respond, "these are delicious." She took another sip and looked at me, patient.

"I worked for a man, a few years ago. In Seattle." I surprised myself, starting with Coop instead of explaining my history with Chance.

"Benjamin Cooper," Chava said.

"You remember his name?"

"Of course I do. He took you in, gave you a purpose. You looked up to him. I could tell from when you talked about him."

"I didn't think I talked about him that much."

"Sometimes it's not about quantity, it's about quality," Chava said.

I took a deep breath. Maybe my mother already knew more than I thought.

"He killed himself."

"I remember that too," Chava said. "I read about it online. I saw your name in the article."

"You knew? How come you never said anything?"

"I figured you'd tell me when you were ready, or not tell me, if that was what you needed. I knew you were okay … physically, so I didn't need to show up on your doorstep."

Chava waited.

"I can't believe you saw that article from Vegas. It wasn't big news."

"I have a Google Alert attached to your name."

Chava used a Google Alert? For me? I must have looked startled. Because she shrugged. "I give you space; that doesn't mean I don't keep track."

Her interest in my life gave me the courage to continue. "I was with Chance when Coop … when he shot himself."

"And you blame yourself for what he did?"

"I was supposed to go to a Mariner's game with Coop. He loved baseball…" I trailed off, unable to finish.

"And you stood him up to be with the man you loved." The words could have felt harsh, but instead I heard understanding behind Chava's gentle cadence. "You know," she said, "if someone wants to commit suicide, they are going to find the time and place to do it."

"But he wouldn't have done it that day," I said, voicing the guilt I'd carried around with me since it happened. "And maybe he wouldn't have had the courage the next time."

"Were you and Benjamin Cooper romantically involved?"

"No. Never. He was more of a …" I stopped, wondering if Chava would hear it as a slight to her parenting.

"Everyone should have a father figure," she said, "but I hope you can see he would understand you preferring to spend time with Chance over a baseball game with him. You didn't kill him, Edwina, and you couldn't have stopped him."

I sat for a moment, staring out at the street. I'd always known on some level I couldn't have stopped Coop, but what kind of private investigator was I, that I didn't even see it coming?

Did I want to admit that to Chava? If we kept talking, she'd pinpoint everything I didn't want to talk about. I'd never been able to lie to her. Maybe that's why I started clamming up about things.

"He still cares about you," Chava said, returning to our recent encounter with Chance.

"Why do you say that?"

"I can tell," she said, with a toss of her head. "Just by the way he says your name."

Who was I to argue with that?

"So Chance and his partner are investigating Deirdre's death?" Chava said, clearly seeing I had said all I could on the topic of Benjamin Cooper and Chance Parker for the time being.

"They are. Unfortunately, they don't seem to want to keep me in the loop."

"I doubt that's personal," she said, patting me on the hand.

I had to admit it was nice to have told someone at least part of what I was going through.

We finished our mochas and I stood up. I was done talking about the past and worrying about the future.

"Let's go look for Kendra," I said, thinking to myself, *Maybe her I can save.*

A FEW HOURS LATER FOUND us headed south to the Samish River Casino. Despite living in the area for several years, I'd never found a reason to visit. I knew where it was, of course; it was hard to miss. Fifteen minutes out of B'ham, the casino appeared on the west side of the freeway. The brightly lit façade of the complex always felt jarring, stuck as it was in the peaceful wooded hills surrounding it, making me steer clear. Plus, I'd never had reason to stop. Gambling was Chava's domain, not mine. The complex boasted three hotels, four restaurants, twenty gaming tables, and a veritable sea of slot machines. The sprawling glitz of the casino was totally alien to me. Pulling into the parking lot, I already felt like a fish out of water.

The bright red roof encircled by the big round lights of a theatrical marquee flashed despite the daylight hours. The parking lot, almost larger than the entire area of downtown B'ham, was more than half full, even though it was not yet noon. An enormous LED screen emphasized all the fun I would be missing in the near future—including the casino's New Year's Eve bash, which highlighted a band I remembered from the '80s. The band members' pictures flashed on the screen, long hair carefully dyed and styled to hide receding hairlines, and bodies looking a few pounds heavier than I remembered from my youth.

Nostalgia tempted me to buy a ticket, but I knew the feeling wouldn't last.

"Ready, Eddie?" Chava asked with a grin.

"Seriously? Now you're going to start rhyming my name?"

"What? I remembered not to call you Edwina."

I had to give her credit for that.

After locking up my car, we trotted across the parking lot toward the front entrance. The weather was cold and a slight rain had started to fall. At least it would be warm and dry inside. Music piped out of speakers inset into the façade. Nostalgia appeared to be the mood of the day. Billy Squire needed me to know that everybody wants me. I had a momentary flashback to Chava playing that record twenty-five years ago. She'd jump around the house singing into a hairbrush, gyrating like the best of them. MTV had nothing on Chava.

I looked over at her, ready to share a moment from our history, still a little warm and fuzzy from our intimate conversation earlier, but she was already disappearing inside.

The thrall of the casino had taken over, turning my mother into a card shark I barely recognized.

The interior was dark; the absence of windows kept the players from tracking how many hours they'd been inside. Neon tube lighting stretched around the ceiling, and lights and bells flashed all around us. The sound of coins dropping into slots and the buzz, whir, clicks of the machines played a counterpoint to the occasional ding, ding, ding, of the winners. Vacant-eyed retirees stared at nothing while their arms moved back and forth as if of their own accord.

Hand into the plastic cup, remove a token, reach up and drop it in the slot. Pull the handle. Repeat.

Endlessly.

I'd been here less than a minute and it felt like bugs crawled on my skin.

"Let's go check out the card games," Chava said. Her voice had that professional sound to it again and I could see her features had changed. She looked focused, alert, and maybe slightly manic. I wasn't sure if she was suffering from withdrawal—this had probably been the longest period of time she hadn't played professionally since she moved to Vegas—or if she always looked this way at work.

First, she made a beeline for the back of the room, where women worked behind bars and bullet-proof Plexiglas, handing out chips in exchange for cash. I wondered if people found it psychologically easier to lose chips than actual money. I also wondered why anyone would want to work in a windowless room behind bars. Our cashier appeared cheerful enough when she took Chava's money and slid a few stacks of chips across the counter under the pass through. I let Chava lead me into the other room where the card players sat at the blackjack tables.

"Here," she said, handing me some chips. "We'll look a little more like we belong with these in our hands."

Passing a roulette table, I noticed the rips in the brown leather padding around the edges. It was like going to Disneyland and finding peeling paint on Sleeping Beauty's Castle. It felt tawdry, somehow. The table was bigger than I imagined—roughly the length of a regulation pool table but half as wide. It had seen better days, but then, so had most of the people standing around it.

Nothing appealed to me here. I wondered what kept the players chained to the tables, and machines, with a backdrop of nothing but the constant clang of lost change. The room smelled of ancient cigarettes and grease, though I think the odor came from the inhabitants, not the room itself. There was no smoking inside. Only the casinos on reservations permitted that habit anymore. The restaurants were too far away to be contributing to the smell.

"Let's just wait here a minute," Chava said, sitting down at a bar on the far end of the room. Various sporting events played on the TV screens above the rows of liquor bottles. The waitress looked our way and walked over to see what we were drinking. Chava ordered a martini on the rocks.

"What?" she said to me as I gave her a look. "I'm just staying in character."

I didn't want to know what character she was staying in, so I just asked for a soda with a twist.

The waitress brought us our drinks, and at least Chava paid for hers. She took a sip and sighed. I could tell she missed "the life." Swinging around on her barstool, she sat with her back to the bar and surveyed the tiny kingdom like a soon-to-be conqueror sizing up the opposing team.

"Don't be obvious, cookie, but look over your left shoulder," Chava said out of the corner of her mouth.

"Don't be obvious? You're talking like we're in a 1940s film noir and I'm the one you're worried about being obvious?"

"Just humor me," she said.

I pretended to stretch my back, as if telegraphing the weariness I felt from hours of sitting in front of a card table or slot machine. Twisting from side to side, I got a look at the object of Chava's interest.

Vincent Careno. I recognized him from the picture Chava had brought up on the Internet.

He sat in profile to us, his bodyguard leaning against the wall behind him. Careno was handsome in a dark, swarthy, reptilian kind of way. His hair glinted in the neon lights of the casino, the effect of some no doubt expensive hair pomade. The bodyguard was built like a woolly mammoth with an equal amount of hair. Fuzz spilled out of his sleeves and reached for his fingers, which twitched every few moments like he was just dying to pull out his gun and take somebody down. Careno, on the other hand, appeared totally relaxed, with several stacks of chips sitting in front of him. He looked ensconced for the duration.

"What's with Sasquatch?" I asked.

"Be nice. It's not his fault."

"What's not his fault?"

"Hypertrichosis."

"What?"

"It's a genetic condition that causes an unusual growth of hair."

"You're serious?"

"It's often considered the reason the werewolf myth came about."

"How do you know this stuff?"

"I get curious about something, I ask questions."

Maybe I got my investigative gene from my mother.

"Okay. I promise not to call him Sasquatch. So what do we do now?" I asked instead.

"Do you want to make him talk? Or just shadow him and see if he leads us to the missing dame?"

My mother the gumshoe.

"You're having way too much fun here, Chava."

"Maybe you should call me Mom."

I sputtered out my mouthful of soda water. "What?"

"Maybe you should call me Mom."

"You never wanted me to call you that, ever. Why start now?"

"Maybe I shouldn't have made you call me Chava when you were a kid."

"Seriously? I thought you'd be even more excited to have people think we're sisters now that I'm over thirty."

"We are looking more and more like sisters," Chava said. "You really should take better care of your skin."

She wasn't wrong.

"But there's nothing wrong with acknowledging you're my child," Chava continued, "right?" There was something in her voice I couldn't put my finger on. Was that an emotion I heard? Was that longing?

"You would want that?" I asked, surprised at the catch in my throat.

"Hello, Cha-cha," I heard over my shoulder. We'd been so engrossed in our conversation, neither of us had noticed the two men walk up. It didn't hurt that the carpet was as thick as upholstery. Turning around, I found myself face to face with Vincent Careno, who apparently wasn't as ensconced as I'd thought. Hairy Muscle Man now leaned against the edge of the bar.

Cha-cha?

"Hello, Vinnie. How's it going?"

Vinnie?

Stunned, I turned back to see my mother looking at Vincent with a funny lopsided grin on her face.

I'd seen that look before, usually directed at one of my childhood "uncles."

"Who's your pal?" Vincent asked, nodding at me.

"This is Eddie, an old friend of mine," Chava said without batting an eye. So much for calling her Mom.

My day just kept getting weirder.

"Hello, Eddie. Pleased to make your acquaintance," Vincent

said, reaching out to give me a courtly kiss on the back of my hand.

Careno was handsome in an I-could-kill-you-if-I-really-needed-to kind of way. Or have-you-killed, if Chava was right about Careno's specialization as a money launderer, not a killer. Middle-aged, he wore his years well—his physique trim and his hair still black. He looked like the kind of guy who would continue getting better looking as he aged, his features sharpening into something more interesting than his youthful visage had allowed. His dark eyes showed a glint of humor his smile didn't.

"I heard you'd left Vegas rather abruptly, Cha-cha."

There was that name again. This was who my mother was when I wasn't around? A high-stakes gambler who rubbed elbows with nefarious Mafiosi and got black eyes when she was run out of casinos for counting cards? I'd always managed to keep Chava's life compartmentalized. If I visited her, she took time off, so I'd never gone to a casino with her before. When she came to visit me, we did touristy things, like the Space Needle in Seattle or one spectacularly misguided skiing trip to Whistler B.C. Apparently neither Chava nor I have any business trying to learn that particular sport; maybe it's a Jewish thing. Were there any professional Jewish skiers? I'd have to look that up.

But I'd never actually spent too much time thinking about the day-to-day of her life without me. It had always been easier not to know. I wondered if she felt the same about me. Her interest in my career felt newfound, but after the "Mom" revelation, maybe I had misjudged her.

If nothing else, it was clear I didn't really know her.

"Time for something new, Vinnie. You can understand that. What brings you here?"

Vincent rocked his head on his shoulders, whether to stretch muscles tired from sitting in a casino or buy time to answer I couldn't tell.

"A little business, a little pleasure," he finally responded vaguely. "And you? Is this work or pleasure for you?"

"Vacation. Pure vacation."

"Looks a lot like your day job," Vinnie said with a laugh. "Well, nice to see you. And nice to meet you, Eddie," he said, nodding to me as he started to return to his table.

"I think we have a mutual friend," I said, deciding to put my cards on the table and see what happened. I figured we were safe in such a public venue.

"Oh? And who might that be?"

"Kendra Hallings."

Vincent stopped in his tracks, then turned slowly, looking at Chava first before his eyes flicked over to me again.

"Hallings, you say?" Vincent said. "I don't think I know any Kendra."

"Maybe you know her husband?"

"I think you must be mistaken."

He turned on his heel and walked back to his table without looking at us again.

"Cha-cha?" I asked.

"What? You can go by Eddie, but I can't have a nickname?"

"I just never thought about you as a Cha-Cha."

"Can we get back to what's important here?"

"He's your friend," I said, "and given the look on your face, maybe a little more than that?"

"What? How can you think that? I have never gotten involved with Vincent. Our relationship is strictly professional."

"Well. On a strictly professional level, was he telling the truth about not knowing Kendra?"

"My best guess is he's lying about Hallings, but not about Kendra."

"Why do you say that?"

"Well, we know he's lying about Hallings, since Hallings owes him money, but he appeared genuinely confused when you said *Kendra* Hallings. My guess is he doesn't know the wife. Or didn't think you'd ask about her."

"How good are you at reading people?" I asked, though I already had a pretty good idea.

"Almost as good as reading cards."

"Well, it's a bit inconclusive, but for now, let's assume you're right and Vincent doesn't know Kendra or have her body stashed somewhere. What now?" I mused out loud.

"Let's have an early lunch. I'm buying," Chava said, surprising me with her continued generosity. "I just need to cash my chips back in, since we already blew our low profile, unless you want to stay and watch me play a few games?"

"Lunch sounds good."

"Okay, but you don't know what you're missing."

Chava and I walked through the casino so she could cash her chips back in and started to ask me which restaurant I wanted to have lunch. Before I could get an answer out, I saw Chava's eyes go wide. A hulking shadow appeared out of nowhere and wrapped itself around her.

"Mr. Careno would like a word with both of you. Privately."

Careno's bodyguard had Chava's arm in a lock that looked simultaneously intimate and terrifying. It was hard to tear my eyes away from the fur snaking out at the sleeves and neck of his expensive and clearly custom-made suit. You can't buy suits and shirts that wide off the rack.

I didn't think he'd physically attack either of us here in the crowded casino, but then, I'd never been face to face with Mob muscle before. I also noticed he'd grabbed Chava when we were the farthest from other people. No one stood in our immediate proximity, and I wondered how much damage he could do before help arrived.

"I'd hate to hurt your mother," the Mob muscle said. I could see surprise in Chava's face as she realized Vincent Careno knew exactly who I was.

I guess *Mom* didn't read people so good after all.

Chapter Twenty

WE TURNED AND MOVED WITH Muscles toward the elevators. I'd decided to go along with him instead of fighting it out right there on the floor. After all, I'd lose. We must have made an odd trio, the big man holding Chava as if in a passionate embrace. From a distance, it probably looked like he just had his arm around her. I remained slightly separate, a third wheel to their romantic liaison.

We went up to the top floor without speaking—Chava's eyes downcast on the carpet, Muscle Man's straight ahead. I kept my attention glued to the Hulk. I could see he shaved parts of his face. His hair grew excessively there too. His five o'clock shadow started at his hairline and ended at his moustache, with the hair already roughing in, even though it wasn't yet noon. The elevator dinged and we stepped out in unison, Chava and Beastman in front, me walking behind like a well-behaved German Shepard. Fuzzy Muscles seemed to know I wouldn't leave Chava alone with him; he never even looked my way.

Walking down the plush, carpeted hallway, a delicate light blue that belied the nature of the building we were in, we stopped in front of the door at the far end. The bodyguard swiped a keycard and the door swung open to reveal a large suite. Vincent stood at a small minibar, pouring himself a drink. Did everyone drink this early in the day in Chava's world? He didn't turn as we entered, but caught Chava's eyes in the mirror above the bar as we came into the room.

"Drink, Cha-cha?"

"Don't mind if I do," she said, her voice still in the strange register she had used since we walked in the front door of the casino.

"Eddie?" Vincent began to make a martini for Chava without asking what she'd have.

"Sure, since we're all getting chummy."

"What would you like?"

"Vodka on the rocks, if you would be so kind."

The time for soda with a twist had passed.

Muscles stepped back away from Chava, but stood between the door and us. I figured he was probably packing, so even if either of us could get through the wall of flesh he posed, we still might not make it out.

"Pat her down," Vincent said to his hairy henchman. "You understand, don't you, Eddie?"

I put my arms out and stood with a wider stance. No use poking the bear. "Just like getting through airport security, right?" I said to demonstrate my acquiescence. "At least you aren't using a scatter machine to see me naked."

I swore the bodyguard hid a smile at that one.

"Your daughter has a sense of humor," Vincent said to Chava as he handed her a martini and went to pour my drink.

"She gets that from me," Chava said. I couldn't read anxiety in her voice, so I wondered if she wasn't scared or was a better actor than I gave her credit for. After all, she did maintain a poker face for a living.

Muscles performed the pat down on me in a fast, professional manner. TSA could actually learn a thing or two from the man. He nodded to Vincent I wasn't carrying or wired.

"No offense meant by the intrusion," Vincent said to me. "It's not personal."

"None taken," I said as I took the drink he handed over.

The bodyguard looked from Chava to Vincent, raising an eyebrow in question.

"Be gentle with me," Chava said, holding her arms out so he could frisk her. She didn't even put down her drink.

"Why don't we all sit a moment and chat," Vincent said when the bodyguard was finished. Not waiting for our response, he moved over to the seating area in the suite. Vincent sat on a chair, relegating Chava and me to the matching loveseat. We sat down together. The Fuzz went back to his post by the door.

"*L'Chaim,*" he said, raising his glass.

"*L'Chaim,*" Chava said in response.

I just sipped and kept my eyes on Vincent.

I'm such a rebel.

"Why don't you tell me a little bit about your relationship with Matthew Hallings," Vincent said, looking at me.

"I don't have any relationship with Matthew Hallings," I said.

"Excuse me," Vincent said, setting his highball glass down on an end table. "Your relationship with Kendra Hallings."

"What's it to you?"

Vincent tsk-tsked and looked at Chava again. "Your daughter isn't very polite, is she?"

"That she must get from her father," Chava said. Vincent chuckled, but said nothing. Chava had always blamed my long-absent father for my transgressions.

"How did you know Eddie's my daughter?"

"Cha-cha, I know everything about the regulars in Vegas. You play far too much poker, and win far too many hands, for me not to have checked you out. I like to know where a person's weaknesses may lie."

"Are you threatening my child?" Chava said, half rising from her seat as if she might take the mobster on barehanded right then and there.

"Relax for a moment, would you?" Vincent said, the amusement I'd seen earlier in his eyes finally reaching his mouth. The corners of his lips twitched and I thought he was holding back a smile. "I said I liked to know what they are, I didn't say I'd ever use them. Why would I threaten your daughter?"

"Well, then, what is this, Vinnie? You have your trained monkey there ..." she turned and looked at Muscles standing at the door behind us. "No offense."

"None taken," the trained monkey said. My, weren't we a polite group?

"You have your trained monkey waylay us on our way to a nice lunch and bring us up here under threat of physical violence, pat us down, and now you have apparently checked me out? What am I supposed to think?"

"Really?" Vincent said, speaking over our heads at Muscles. "Did you really use the threat of physical violence?" The big man shrugged, his expression unchanged.

"Chava. Trust me when I say no one is going to hurt either you or your daughter."

"So we could just up and walk away?" Chava asked.

"You could, but I don't think you want to," Vincent said, picking up his glass again and taking another sip.

"And why not?" Chava asked, standing up. "Why shouldn't we just walk right out of here?"

"Because he knows where Kendra is," I said, watching Vincent closely. Something wasn't adding up in this conversation. "Don't you, Vincent?"

He swung his coal-black eyes toward me, that humor glinting in them again.

"Is she missing?" he asked.

"Don't play games. Hallings is in to you for a lot of money. Do you have his wife or not?"

Vincent put his glass back down with a decisive thump, his countenance changed, as if he'd made up his mind about something.

"What do you think?" he said, loud enough for someone in the bedroom to hear. "Do you want to join the conversation?"

Another man stepped into the room. Chava gasped and her face went white.

"Who is this?" I asked her, as she clearly knew the man hiding out in the gangster's hotel room.

She said his name just before she dropped down in a dead faint.

I might have fainted myself if Chava hadn't beaten me to it.

Chapter Twenty-One

———•———

I'D HEARD THE NAME EDUARDO Zapata my entire life. Just as she'd blamed my father when I was impolite to Vincent Cardeno earlier, I'd heard "you must get that from the Zapata side" every time I'd misbehaved as a child. As a firm believer in nurture over nature, I thought Chava should take some responsibility for the more challenging aspects of my personality.

Looking at the man who'd given me half my chromosomes, however, I realized nature might have a little more to do with things than I'd originally believed. He had my build and I could see where I got my hair color. In fact, the face I couldn't stop staring at explained every one of my features.

"Hi, Dad," I said. What else should one say when meeting one's father for the first time as an adult?

"I'm good, I'm okay. No one worry about me," Chava said as she struggled to sit up from where she'd fallen back on the sofa.

I went over to her and grabbed her arm, taking her pulse. It was fast, but strong.

"You'll live. Let me get you a glass of water."

"Sit, Eddie," Vincent said. "Lonnie will get that."

Lonnie? The muscle man's name was Lonnie? I guess with a physique like his no one was going to make fun of him. Or maybe he worked so hard at his physical prowess because he'd been bullied as a kid.

Lonnie walked over and poured Chava a glass of water. My father moved a chair over from where it sat near the window and joined our little group. Chava and I now sat flanked on either side by Vegas Mafiosi, or whatever my father was.

I was starting to wish I'd let the whole Kendra business go.

"So," I said, looking at my father, "what's new?"

Eduardo smiled at me. "Eddie. I've been wanting to meet you, but I never pictured our reunion quite like this."

His voice was low pitched, soft. It carried well, but I found myself leaning forward slightly so I didn't miss anything.

This guy was good.

"So what's the word on Kendra Hallings?" I said.

Eduardo laughed and looked at Vincent, volumes of information shuttled between them. The image of Chance and his partner Kate communicating the same way rose up in my mind's eye; I quickly quashed it, not wanting to be distracted from the situation at hand.

"You're single-minded in your purpose, *mija*."

"If you've got her, I'd like her back," I said, ignoring the reference he made to our familial relationship, "Otherwise I'll just be on my way."

"Thank you," Chava said to Lonnie, taking the water glass. She began to sip slowly, her eyes focused on some distant horizon, as if none of us existed at all.

A silence settled on the room. Lonnie also stared off into space at his own private movie screen. I wondered for a moment what a guy like that thought about. New ways to kill without leaving a mark? Maybe I was being unfair. He could be writing poetry in his head for all I knew. Or designing a new hair removal product.

"You never introduced us," I finally said to Chava, gesturing toward Eduardo, "When I came out to Vegas to visit you."

"I haven't seen your father since …." Chava blushed. It may have been the first time in my life I saw my mother embarrassed.

Not wanting to hear details about her sexual escapades, especially with the man in question not only in the room, but my long absent father, I shifted the subject back to Kendra.

"So about Mrs. Hallings—"

"We have no idea as to the whereabouts of this Kendra Hallings," Eduardo said.

"But Matthew Hallings does owe you something close to the tune of half a million dollars," I said. "Which I assume is gathering interest by the day."

"Our dealings with Mr. Hallings are really none of your concern," Vincent said.

Boy, these guys could say mundane things in a conversational tone and still make me wonder if I was going to get out of the room alive.

"But Kendra is," I said, wearing the false bravado on my sleeve like a flag.

"Why are you so concerned about this woman?" my father asked.

"She's my client. She's missing. I just want to know if she's okay."

"And she owes Eddie money," Chava said, then giggled. "Eddie Money, get it? Like the singer?"

Chava has a habit of saying totally inappropriate things when she's nervous. I wondered if her nerves were from our being in actual physical danger from the Mob or the presence of my father, who apparently worked for the Vegas Mafia too.

No wonder she never talked about him.

I was having enough trouble focusing at the moment myself. I started to ask her how she got involved with Eduardo Zapata in Spokane, Washington, of all places, but realized this was not the time or the place.

It was all a bit much.

Eduardo smiled again, raising the hairs on the back of my neck. "Ah, she doesn't pay you, so you go after her. I understand that completely. We aren't so different, Edwina."

Great, now I had two people using that name.

"Eddie," I said.

"Eddie," he repeated and the smile disappeared. I couldn't decide which expression was worse.

"Look, Chava and I don't want to be any trouble to you. I don't care what your deal is with Hallings. You're right, he's not my concern. But, if you've got Kendra stashed around here someplace, why not just hand her over and we'll be on our way? I'm sure you've got other leverage for Hallings. I don't even need to let him know Kendra's with me."

Eduardo looked at me for a very long moment. His face was impassive; only his eyes were alight with something that might have been interest, or maybe they always looked like that—as if a pilot light glowed inside him, ready to start a fire in an instant if the situation called for one.

"Edwina," he finally said, "out of respect for your mother, and because you are my daughter. I'm going to give you one free pass here. We do not have Kendra. It's none of your business, but I will tell you that our dealings with Hallings have been resolved. We never included his wife in any way, that would be … gauche. She may be missing, but it's not our doing. Do you understand me?"

I nodded yes. What else could I do?

"Lonnie will see you out," Vincent said. "You're feeling better, Cha-cha?" he asked, bending over Chava to help her stand. In that moment, when Vincent used an endearment with Chava, I saw a crack in Eduardo's façade. A flicker of expression that said he didn't quite approve. I wondered if he didn't like that another man knew my mother better than he did.

What had happened between these two people? How had they come together just long enough to produce me?

And what had Chava known about him all these years? Her

story had always been that she didn't know where he'd gone or what had happened to him, and that he knew nothing about me.

Had all that been a lie?

Taking my cue from Chava, I stood and walked behind her toward the door, with Lonnie in the lead.

"Edwina," I heard my father's voice behind us. I turned. Would I get a moment of paternal interest? A question about my well-being? A request to meet again?

"You understand what a free pass is, right?" he asked.

"I do."

"And you understand there will not be another one."

I did.

I guess that was it for paternal advice.

SITTING IN MY CAR IN the parking lot, I put my head on the steering wheel and took several deep breaths. I felt pressure on my shoulder blade, and realized Chava was stroking my back like you would a sick child.

It felt good.

"What the hell was that, Cha-cha?" I asked bolting upright and getting my indignation fired up. "Really? Cha-cha? From a mobster? Not to mention my father …."

"Edwina …" she said. I glared. "Eddie," she corrected, "you're upset. I get that. But you've got to believe me. I had no idea your father was here. I had no idea he even knew Vincent. Do you really think I'd bring you here without a word of warning if I did? I'm in shock myself."

One thing I knew about my mother—she liked to control a situation—so no, I didn't think she'd have brought us over here if she'd had any idea what would happen.

"How come you never told me my father worked for the Mafia?"

"I didn't know he worked for the Mafia, Edwina. I haven't seen the man in thirty years."

I let the Edwina slip for the time being. We were both a little tense.

"How does he know about me?" I asked.

"I have no idea."

Looking sharply at her, I could see she was telling the truth. Her tongue never left her mouth, her tell firmly in place. Looking up at the penthouse side of the casino's hotel we'd just exited, I could imagine the room they were in. Vincent Careno, money launderer, and my father—what exactly did he do for them? He was an outsider, not an Italian, but a Latino from Mexico. Like I was, or half was, anyway. If Chava could reconnect to her Jewish roots, should I investigate the part of me from Mexico? It was something I'd never thought about before, despite my looks. I didn't even speak Spanish very well, just a few years in high school and some bits and pieces picked up from living on the West Coast.

I was a failure as a Jew and a Latina. What did that say about me?

Time enough to think about that later. Now I needed to focus on my father as a person of interest, not as half my genetic code. What role did he play with the Vegas crew?

A contract killer or a cleaner seemed the two most obvious choices. Was my father someone who came in and cleared out a crime scene before the police arrived? Like Harvey Keitel in *Pulp Fiction*? Or worse, did he do the actual hitting?

"Do we believe they don't have Kendra?" I asked, shoving thoughts of my father off into a dusty room in my head and slamming the door.

"I do," Chava said. "They don't need to lie to us."

"Why not? If they killed her, they certainly weren't going to announce it to us."

"Because if they had Kendra, they never would have taken us upstairs to begin with. We never would have seen them at all."

"Vincent, in the casino. That was a setup."

"I think so. I think they knew when we came in and Eduardo decided he wanted to learn what was up. He had Vincent come down to verify it was us, then Lonnie got us upstairs. He didn't want that reunion happening in a public place."

"How would they know we'd come in?"

"Surveillance, probably. There are cameras all over the casino. Maybe they have access in some way. Or they just got lucky and were looking out the window. Or Vincent saw us when we came in and called up to your father in the room. There's lots of ways we could have been made."

"What kind of trouble did you really get into down in Vegas?" I said, wondering why Chava was suddenly an expert on video surveillance and the activities of mobsters.

Chava fell silent. She looked out the window for a long moment, then got out of the car. Taking a seat on a concrete bench in front of the hotel side of the casino, she pulled a pack of menthols out of her bag. She lit up and took a long drag, eyes closed. She never opened them the whole time she smoked the cigarette down, expertly flicking ashes into a clump of bushes without looking. When she reached the end, she opened her eyes, stubbed it out on the matching concrete ashtray, and tossed the butt inside. Then she walked back to the car, some kind of decision made.

She sat next to me in a haze of menthol smoke and Aqua Net, that familiar smell that took me back to childhood. I could see the younger Chava in the lines of her face and wondered what it had really been like for her, raising a child alone. I knew I was more than just a burden, but that didn't mean it was easy.

"For a private investigator, you certainly never showed any interest in learning about your father," she said, surprising me with her twist in the conversation.

"You always said you didn't know much about him."

"And that kept you from looking into him?"

"I respected your privacy."

"How would I even know you'd done any research? Come

on, Eddie, is that really what kept you from searching for him? I never lied about his name. You chose not to look."

This sat me back in my seat. I'd always believed I didn't look into my father because of what Chava told me. It never occurred to me it was because deep down, I didn't want to know.

What was I afraid of?

That he knew about me and didn't want me? Well, it looked like that was true.

"How did you meet him?" I finally asked, aware I never had before.

"Your grandfather. They worked together."

"Wait, what? Opa introduced you?"

Chava nodded, her eyes unfocused, her mind in the past.

"But if he worked for Opa, that means—"

"Yes," Chava said, tucking her lighter back into her bag, she'd held it in her hand all this time, like a talisman. "Your father was a butcher."

The thought gave me the willies. It meant he was perfectly capable of taking another human being apart, methodically and easily, for disposal.

Maybe he really was a cleaner. How much of my ethics had I inherited from this man?

I sat for a moment thinking about how little I knew about my own family history. On my mother's side, Opa died when I was five. My strongest memory of my grandfather was the blue numbers tattooed on his arm, though it would be years before I understood what they signified.

He immigrated to the United States as soon as he could after his release from Bergen-Belsen, a Sephardic Jew working his way ever westward until he settled in Spokane. There was a history of Jewish immigrants in Eastern Washington. The Native Indian tribes told stories of other "egg-eaters," as they called the white men who wouldn't eat meat, as it wouldn't be kosher.

My grandmother's family relocated to Spokane during the pogroms in Russia in the early 1900s; she was an Ashkenazi Jew. My grandmother's parents disowned her for marrying a Sephardic Jew, though Opa never practiced anything after the war. In solidarity, my grandmother also stopped practicing her religion. My mother was born two years after the wedding, and Chava grew up without learning the traditions of either branch.

Though Opa didn't practice, he did keep his butcher shop kosher, allowing him to sell to the Jewish population, a small but steady customer base. We lived on the edge of the Jewish neighborhood, always outsiders looking in.

Chava had told me how much she hated the shop. The smell of blood, the sight of the carcasses taken apart, piece by piece, the feel of raw meat on her hands. After my grandfather died, she sold the store and began moving from job to job until I left town and she went south.

And the rest, as they say, is history.

"How long did you know him," I asked. "Eduardo. You know, before—"

"Before I got pregnant with you?" she said, that faraway look returning to her eyes. "Not long. A few months. He was so handsome—those dark eyes, all that black hair. That accent. He was different from anyone else I knew. He kind of swept me off my feet."

"Why did you stop seeing each other?"

"He was restless. Back then. Maybe he still is—I don't know. He left me a note. It just said he was leaving town. I found it after I learned I was pregnant with you, but before I had time to tell him. I took it as a sign and let it go."

"Why did you decide to have me? Or keep me?"

"I wasn't sure I would," Chava said, "at first." Her admission was barely audible. "Abortions were legal, and I thought about it. But I kept putting it off. Then I felt you move for the first time. Did you know they call that the quickening? When you start to feel your baby move. I knew then, whatever the sacrifice it was to keep you, it would be worth it."

I wanted to ask if she regretted that choice. But I held my tongue. I'd had enough revelations for one day.

"What now?" Chava finally asked when I didn't acknowledge her confession.

"I'm not sure," I said, shaking off the unexpected trip down memory lane. "With the Mob connection a dead end, I'm not sure where Kendra's gone. Maybe the mysterious male caller really was telling the truth, and she's gone off somewhere on her own. Maybe she fled her marriage when she realized Hallings wasn't worth anything. She also might choose not to have the baby or give it away. None of which is my problem. Maybe it's time I just let the whole thing go."

"But we know there's a killer out there," Chava said. "And Kendra could still be in trouble."

"The police are handling the investigation," I said. "I should probably just leave all of this to them."

I could do that, right?

"I'll take you out to lunch instead," I told Chava. "We'll head over to the Skylark."

I didn't tell her it sat across the street from the Rustic Coffee Bar and that maybe we'd catch a glimpse of Chance Parker. Even if I let the Kendra thing go, the outcome of the investigation into Deirdre's death still mattered to me. I wanted to know who killed her and why, though maybe I wasn't the person who should track that killer down. Chance Parker and Kate Jarek would do their jobs, and when it was finished maybe Chance would be willing to sit down and talk to me.

A girl can dream, right?

Chapter Twenty-Two

———•———

"**Y**OU KNOW I CAN'T TALK about it," Chance said, as we stood outside the coffee bar. Kate sat in a parked car writing notes while Chance picked up their drinks. Even if I didn't already know the two detectives had been working nonstop, I could tell by the fatigue in Chance's face.

"No, of course not. I was really just asking how *you're* doing," I said.

Chance looked over at Chava, who'd stepped back a little after saying hello.

"It's been quite the introduction to Bellingham," he said, including both of us in his response.

"When did you move here?" Chava asked. "I understand it hasn't been long."

"Just a week ago," he said. "They only get a few homicides a year. I wasn't expecting this kind of investigation so soon. All I've discovered about my new city so far is where to get the best coffee."

"When things calm down I'd be happy to show you around," I said, the words leaving my mouth before I could stop myself. How bad was I going to feel if he said no?

He looked at me a beat longer than I would have liked before answering, but his noncommittal "We could do that," made my heart soar just a little.

It was better than no, right?

Chava patted my arm as we watched him climb into the driver's seat. "That was a yes," Chava said. "Even if it didn't sound like one. Let's get some lunch. I think we can both use a timeout from the men in our past."

Leaving all the complicated stuff behind for the rest of the day, we spent a quiet night playing cards and watching TV. I turned in early, tired from three restless nights without enough sleep.

Let it go, I told myself before I drifted off. *Let it all go. Things have been over with Chance for two years. It's crazy to think he's still got feelings for you. And you've lived this long without your father in the picture. Why do you want to get to know him now? Especially given his line of work.* These thoughts faded as sleep overtook me.

But letting go wasn't to be.

The shrill of my cellphone brought me out of a sound sleep.

"Eddie Shoes," I said, struggling to wake up. Calls in the middle of the night were never good news.

"Eddie? It's me, Kendra."

"Where the hell have you been?" I asked. "Everyone's—"

The sound of Kendra sobbing cut off my words. This time I knew it was genuine. Her fear climbed through my cell and grabbed hold of the back of my neck.

"What is it? Are you hurt? Are you all right?" I said.

Kendra continued to sob, though I could tell she was trying to speak.

"I …"—sob—"I …"—sob—"need help." Was all I managed to make out through the strangled sounds she made.

"Kendra, listen to me. Calm down. Take a breath." I could hear her taking deep breaths. "Where are you?"

"I'm not totally sure," she said between large gulps of air.

"Are you hurt?"

"No. Not really."

I decided the "not really" couldn't be that bad or I'd hear pain in her voice, not just fear.

"Is someone holding you?"

"Yes."

"Is he there with you?"

"No. But he's coming back."

"Get out now and call me again when you're safe."

"I don't know how to get out. I'm locked in."

"And you don't know where you are?"

"No."

"And you're in danger from this man?"

"I think he might kill me."

The cellphone she was on should have GPS, but I had no way of knowing what the number was to trace, and it could be a burner cell with no way of determining the owner. Contacting the police to trace the call would take time I didn't know if Kendra had. Just when I thought it couldn't get worse, I heard a beeping sound.

"What's that?" I asked.

"I think the cellphone is going dead," Kendra said, the panic rising in her voice.

"Okay. Think fast. Tell me everything you can about where you've been taken. The vehicle you were moved in. Do you know who he is?"

"His name is Christopher Leeds. He drives a silver Lexus." Kendra paused a moment and I heard the low battery beep again.

"Hurry, Kendra, what else can you remember? Are you still in Bellingham?"

"We drove about half an hour after we left his house." That sounded like she went willingly. If that was true, why was she in danger now? And wasn't that a silver Lexus I saw her get into outside my office Thursday afternoon?

"His house? You were at his house? Voluntarily?"

"Yes. Don't be mad at me."

I decided I could be mad later, after I knew the whole story.

"Where's his house?" I asked instead, thinking it might give me a place to start looking for Kendra. She gave me an address not too far away.

"Couldn't you see where he went—after you left his house?"

"I was in the trunk."

"He stuffed you in there?" I asked, wondering if she'd done something to anger him that caused him to turn on her.

"No. We didn't want anyone to see me."

"And then what happened?" I asked.

"We arrived inside some kind of warehouse. I got out, but nothing was what I expected."

What had she expected?

"You've got to help me, Eddie. Me and my baby."

The cellphone Kendra called from chose that moment to give up the ghost, and her voice went dead in my hand.

Cursing, I extricated myself from the sheets, blankets, and comforter that had entangled me when I struggled to answer the phone. I got up and made my way to the kitchen, where my laptop sat from earlier that evening.

Apparently I wasn't done with my search for Kendra Hallings.

I'd just gotten it turned on and connected to the Internet when Chava's door opened and she padded into the kitchen.

"What's going on?" she asked, rubbing sleep from her eyes.

"Kendra," I said, clicking away on my keyboard. I wanted to see what I could learn about this Christopher Leeds as fast as I could.

"She called?" Chava said, plunking down across from me at the table. "Is she all right?"

I brought her up to speed while I typed, finding little about any Christopher Leeds in Bellingham, only that he did have a silver Lexus registered to the address Kendra had given me.

I debated about doing a further check on him; perhaps he owned property under a "doing business as." But a part of me just wanted to do something more active.

Chava got up and started making coffee with the beans I'd brought home yesterday. "I'll get dressed and we'll head over to the address she gave you," she said.

"First off, you aren't coming with me, and second, you aren't coming with me."

"Don't argue with your mother. You need backup. Two heads are better than one."

"This address is a residence. Kendra said he had her in a warehouse. So it isn't even where she's being held. I do not need backup. And ..." I raised my hand to stop her from interrupting. "And if I did, it would be from the police or a trained professional. We don't know what we're dealing with here, and I can't look out for you."

"You don't need to look out for me," she said, pouring a cup of coffee and putting it down in front of me. "Drink your coffee while I make toast."

"Chava! I don't need toast."

"You do. You can't work on an empty stomach."

As if to prove her right, my stomach chose that moment to growl. I looked at the clock on my computer screen and saw it was 3:00 in the morning. Chava started to bustle around in the kitchen.

"What I should do," I said, "is call the police and let them handle it."

"You could call your friend about it," she said without looking up from the counter where she was popping bread into the toaster. She clearly meant Chance, not Iz. Chava knew I didn't want to call Chance and this would increase the chances I'd bring her along with me.

I spent a moment stewing. Should I contact him now, before I got pulled any further into this mess? Would I be hindering the police investigation if I didn't? What did I know at this point?

I knew that Kendra was alive and claimed to be held against her will, but I also knew Kendra lied. The possibility that I would report her kidnapped to the police only to find out she was fine and just looking for my attention for some reason was pretty darn high.

This would make me look foolish and waste the detectives' time. I was already on thin ice with Chance Parker after how I left Seattle. If I wanted to repair our relationship, that wouldn't help at all.

I also knew someone killed Deirdre and stuffed her body into a wall, which might be connected to Matthew Hallings owing the Mafia a lot of money. But I had no proof his financial situation had any connection to Deirdre; in fact, given the relatively calm conversation I'd had with Mr. Careno and my father, there didn't appear to be anything to report to the police about that either. I certainly didn't want to put my mother on the spot, having to explain how she knew the Mafia or who her connections were in Vegas.

"Do you really think they're going to find Kendra before this Leeds comes back?" Chava said. "And what, hurts her? Kills her? What can the police do you can't?"

"Legally enter properties with search warrants for starters," I said.

"How fast are they going to respond to this? Kendra told you she went willingly."

"The woman called me because she's trapped," I said. "The police would take that seriously regardless of how it started out." I didn't share my idea with Chava that Kendra could be lying to me; that would just give her ammunition.

"But how long will those search warrants take?"

I had mixed feelings about skirting the law. For the most part, I didn't do anything illegal. I followed procedures in my investigations. I drew a line between the type of people

I followed around for my job and myself, preferring to think there was a difference between us. Besides, I liked law enforcement. Even if I didn't want to bother Chance Parker, he wasn't the only detective in town. But Chava had a point: the wheels of justice turned slowly and I didn't have much to go on. Combine that with the other complications, and I could justify my continued investigation without contacting Chance or his partner Kate. It might piss him off, but I wasn't doing anything illegal.

Or at least, less illegal than going into Matthew Hallings's house with Chava. So my present behavior showed a marked improvement.

As much as I didn't trust Kendra, I also didn't want her hurt, and if she needed my help, I should give it to her. Plus, there was an unborn child in the middle of all of this. I wouldn't usually get caught up with that, except Chava's revelations about her feelings for me shifted things. Maybe my mother was right and Kendra could change. And even though I now knew she wasn't an innocent damsel in distress, there was still something about her that made me want to protect her.

Maybe it was just her resemblance to my old high school friend, though that friendship had ended badly; I should only use it as a cautionary tale, not a reason to help her.

"The residential address is the only clue you have, right?" Chava said, no doubt reading into my body language I was starting to cave.

"Yes. The car is registered to the same address."

"So let's just start there. You said she can't be held there. How dangerous could it be to take me with you?"

"He could be there now."

"So we follow him, and he'll lead us to Kendra. I could be your wheel man."

"I've seen how you drive."

"Be nice. I've made you a sandwich." She handed me a turkey on rye, lightly toasted. "See, I've already got your back."

How could I argue with that?

"All right, you win. Let's go."

Despite my assurance to Chava I didn't anticipate trouble, I thought I better bring my gun. Telling Chava I'd just be a minute to change my clothes, I collected my Colt .45 and tucked it into my holster. With all the heavy winter clothing I was wearing, not even Chava would notice the slight bulge it created, though I'd either have to leave my outerwear unbuttoned or have my gun hopelessly mired in goose down and Gore-Tex. Zipping up my coat, I decided I wouldn't need direct access to my weapon while driving around.

Just what had Kendra gotten into? And was it related to the death of Deirdre Fox? Maybe whatever Chava and I found tonight would answer those questions, for better or worse. And I could solve the case and hand it over to Chance Parker.

That would be an olive branch even he couldn't ignore.

Chapter Twenty-Three

—•—

THE ADDRESS KENDRA GAVE ME was located near the north end of Grand Street. A modest, single-story house set back on a large lot. The house was barely visible from the street, with just the top of the roofline sticking out above unkempt bushes that lined a tall fence between the residence and the street. What I could see looked gray in the pale light of the waning crescent moon. In addition to the bushes around the property, overgrown trees clumped together, their tangled limbs blocking the house as well. They looked like apple trees or some other fruit, their latticework of branches making a good shield despite their leaflessness this time of year. Combined with the tall evergreens between his house and the neighbors', Leeds lived in relative isolation.

As the only car on the road this early in the morning, I didn't want to draw attention to us, so I continued past and went around the corner to park.

"What now?" Chava said. "Should we break in and see what clues might lead us to where he's keeping Kendra?"

"What is it with you breaking into people's houses? Just

because Hallings left his back door open doesn't mean we'll be able to just waltz into Leeds's place."

"So we find another way to get in."

I didn't answer her as I scoped out the street where I'd parked. A few porch lights were on, but the houses themselves were dark. The streetlights were set far apart, keeping the sidewalks mostly in shadow. I rolled the window down and listened. The neighborhood was quiet in the cold, pre-dawn hours of a winter morning.

"You stay here. I'm going to go see if anyone's home."

"I'm not staying here."

"Chava, if you want to be my backup, you have to stay where you can actually do that—back me up. If I don't come back in thirty minutes call the police."

"And tell them what? My daughter broke into someone's house and hasn't returned? That will get you in trouble."

"I'd rather be in trouble than dead. And you don't have to tell them anything about me. Just tell them you think you saw someone breaking into Leeds's address and get them to investigate a possible burglary. Tell them you think you heard gunshots; that will get their attention."

"They'll have your phone number if I call 911."

"I know that. But this is the best I can do. Just take my cell. If I'm not back here at," I looked at my watch, "four fifteen, call 911 and tell them what I told you."

"This would be a lot easier if I had a cellphone too."

"We'll talk about that when this is all over," I said, not wanting to admit she was right. I got out of the car and checked to confirm that my penlight worked and my Swiss army knife was stashed in my zippered pocket. It had everything from a small blade to a corkscrew in case I needed to serve wine and cheese at some point in this adventure. Even better, I patted my gun through my coat for reassurance before I walked around the corner toward Leeds's place. I unbuttoned my coat for easy access to my weapon, though I hoped it wouldn't come to that.

I'd noticed an alley behind the house, so I turned in there and got to the fence in back without mishap. I paused for a moment to listen again and still heard nothing. No lights were on in the alley, and the darkness made me feel less obvious than being on the street.

A fence encircled Leeds's property, with a small, detached single-car garage facing the alley. Peering over the fence, I could see a picnic table in one corner, but other than that, it appeared empty. A concrete path led up to the door and a mudroom was attached to the back of the house. The small, glassed-in porch didn't look hard to get into. The actual door to the house would have more complicated locks. Even so, the back door was less exposed than climbing over the fence in front, so it was my best bet.

The fence around the property was roughly five feet high. I took ahold of the top of it with my hands and gave it a shake to see how solid it felt. The boards threatened to fall over completely under my weight. With nothing around to stand on, climbing over would be awkward. I didn't relish the prospect of collapsing in a heap of old lumber, impaling myself with rusty old nails and giving away my presence before I even got to the house.

Thinking I might be able to enter through the freestanding garage and into the yard, I twisted the handle on the garage door to see if it was locked. It was.

I had on a pair of thick gloves, which wouldn't allow me to do the delicate work required to pick a lock, but I also had on a pair of silk gloves underneath—not so much for warmth as to keep from leaving fingerprints. Taking the thick outer gloves off, I could feel the cold air working to turn my digits into fingersicles.

Pulling lock picks out of my pocket, I clenched the penlight between my teeth to illuminate the garage door handle. I vowed never to let Chava know about my lock picking skills— she'd want me to teach her and I didn't want to encourage her newfound enthusiasm for breaking and entering.

Of course, she might already know how to pick locks. Maybe that was how she really got us into Hallings's house the other night. A line of thought I didn't want to pursue.

The locking mechanism on the handle was simple, and I had it open in less than thirty seconds. Shoving my picks back into my pocket, I stayed crouched at the door, listening again. I didn't hear anything in the quiet night, so I decided my tiny light and illicit behavior had gone unnoticed.

Slowly edging the rolling door up, I waited for the loud screech that would undoubtedly be forthcoming, especially if the door wasn't opened very often. Residents didn't usually use old garages like this one for storing their cars, preferring to park out front and relegating the old structure to storage.

The door started to squeak just after it got high enough for me to slide underneath, so I stopped raising it and rolled inside the garage. Flashing the light around quickly, I ascertained the absence of a car. The chinks in the walls made the temperature the same inside as it was outside. The room was basically empty except for a washer and dryer against one wall.

I muscled the door back down and checked my watch. Twenty-five minutes before Chava called the police. I should have given myself more time, but a tight deadline would keep me motivated.

The door into the yard wasn't locked and I pushed it open and walked toward the back of the house. With no interior lights on, and no sign of the Lexus parked out front, it appeared Leeds wasn't home, which could be bad luck for Kendra if he'd returned to wherever he had her stashed, but good luck for me.

Reaching the door to the mudroom, I turned the knob and found it locked as well. After assessing the lock, I pulled out a credit card I used for just such purposes. The name on the card wasn't mine, in case it got left behind anywhere; it was one of those fake cards the credit card company sends out with their pleas for application. I slipped it between the door jam and the door, manipulating the catch to swing open. Stepping inside the porch, I pulled the door shut behind me and crouched down.

From my low vantage point, I would be invisible from the outside, should anyone else be creeping around the property in the dead of night. Leaning against the back door, I waited for any movement from inside. I didn't expect any human beings to be sitting in the dark on the other side of the door, but I didn't want to be surprised by any canine inhabitants. Better to know now rather than after I got inside. I scratched at the back door. Unlikely to wake anyone, but I should get a response if Fido lived there too.

After a moment of continued silence, I had reason to hope my little theory held true, and Leeds didn't own a big, highly trained Rottweiler. I decided to chance it. If there wasn't a dangerous guard dog on the other side, I still had Chava poised to call the cops in less than half an hour.

The lock to the house wasn't much harder than the one to the garage, and I soon found myself standing in the kitchen. The house had an air of abandonment, and although my hunch that no one was home was unscientific, it gave me confidence. I moved quickly through the house, my coat unzipped should immediate access to my weapon become necessary. A hunch was one thing, a Smith and Wesson was something altogether more reliable.

At least, the gun was; I was less sure about myself.

I risked turning a light on. The second bedroom clearly served as an office and it seemed a good place to start looking for clues about where Leeds might have Kendra. Leaning against the wall was one of those ugly brown suitcases. It sure looked like it would fill the missing spot in the set we'd seen at the Hallings's place. I had to be in the right house. Unzipping the bag, I found clothes in Kendra's size and style. I didn't think I'd find anything useful, but just in case, I checked through the entire bag.

I found a zippered pouch for cosmetics that felt too heavy to be full of cosmetics. It turned out to be stuffed with cash. Now I was irked. The amount totaled a lot more than she owed me. I stuffed the pouch into my coat pocket as best I could. If I found Kendra, she could have it back minus what was rightfully mine.

Keeping one ear to the ground for Leeds's return and the other for Chava—whom I didn't quite trust to stay put in the car—I got to work.

The innocuous appearance of Leeds's small house must not have piqued her curiosity, because twenty-two minutes later I found her sitting in my driver's seat with my cellphone on her leg.

"Find anything useful?" she asked.

"Maybe. Give me a minute," I said, shoving the pouch into the glove box. Chava shot me a look of curiosity, but she must have sensed my urgency because she didn't ask anything as I began shuffling through the files I'd grabbed from Leeds's home office.

A moment later, I found what I was looking for.

"I think I know where he's got her," I said. "You drive, I'll navigate." I pulled my Thomas Brothers map out from the backseat of my car.

"Don't you have GPS on this thing?" Chava asked as she started up the engine.

"Don't gripe," I replied. "At least I'm letting you drive."

Chapter Twenty-Four

———•———

FROM WHAT I COULD GATHER, Leeds owned real estate under various business holdings. In fact, the only files he appeared to have in his almost empty house were real estate deeds. He had a number of deals going, with both residential and commercial properties. At first I'd thought it would be impossible to sift through all the files to figure out where he might be keeping Kendra, but I could ignore the houses, which made up the majority of the properties. The paperwork for warehouses was neatly filed under W in Leeds's file cabinet.

Riffling through the listings as fast as I could, I found the ones he'd labeled occupied and paying rent and the ones that were empty. It did seem a little weird that all the man had in his file cabinets was information on his properties—no personal information, no credit card bills, no medical records. Now, however, was not the time to think about it.

Turned out Leeds owned the huge vacant warehouses down near the waterfront. It never occurred to me anyone actually owned those buildings; they had been inactive for as long as I could remember. The tan-brick buildings hulked behind tall, chain link fences. Over the years the structures had housed a variety of businesses—lumber mill, a slaughterhouse, a chemical plant. Now they held more broken windows than glass, and their dilapidated appearance brought down the value of the whole area. Plans to renovate came and went. Issues of pollution and the high cost of cleanup compounded the difficulties of launching a major renovation in an economic downturn. For now, the buildings slowly decayed, as ideas for their razing or rebuilding swirled around them.

Few other businesses were open nearby. There was a Puget Sound Energy substation, which ran twenty-four hours a day but employed few people, none of whom were likely to be wandering around in the dark. There was also an old building near the train tracks converted over to offices, but those were all nine-to-five businesses and the occupants wouldn't be around this early in the morning.

Leeds's buildings also had plenty of access doors big enough to drive through, making it easy to transport Kendra inside the building without being seen. And they were far enough away from everything else that she would never be heard even if she could scream for help.

I guided Chava through the still dark streets, not needing the Thomas Brothers once I got us back to a main arterial. It now being closer to 5:00, a few people were out driving around, but the utter darkness of winter kept us anonymous. Bread truck drivers, newspaper delivery personnel, and a few other early morning workers all sped by, too engaged in not spilling their hot coffees in their laps to pay attention to us.

Chava turned off Water Avenue and swung down the side street toward Leeds's property. We could see the large, ramshackle buildings, set back from the road in the concrete sea of a parking lot, halfway to the water. The distinctive orange glow of a low-sodium security light mounted on the largest building lit up the surrounding area. The wide expanse of concrete felt like the length of a football field, though I guessed it was only one hundred feet across. Even if I could get over the fence, I would be horribly exposed while crossing the empty lot—as obvious as a woman breaking out of Purdy Prison.

The place did feel like it should have its own guard tower.

"Why would someone who owned multiple properties live in such a crappy house?" Chava asked.

"Good question. I've been wondering that myself."

"And?"

"And I think we find Kendra first and ask questions about Mr. Leeds later."

"Where do you want me to park?"

I had to admit, Chava didn't have any trouble getting with the program.

"Let's park down there," I said, pointing to another dark warehouse catty corner from where Leeds's buildings sat deteriorating. "Tuck in against the side of that building, where you can see the warehouses but won't be obvious to anyone walking by."

"Does this mean I'm staying in the car again?"

"Yes. You are going to stay here with the cellphone. But instead of a time limit, you're just going to wait. Call the police if anyone else drives up or you hear gunshots or—"

"Gunshots!" she cut me off. "I thought you were exaggerating about actual danger."

"I'll be fine."

"What if you're in trouble inside? A lot can happen to you in there where I can't see you. What if he surprises you? I'll have no way of knowing if—"

"Stop!" I said before she could list any of the things Leeds might do to me if he took me by surprise. "Usually, I have to do this kind of thing with no one waiting on me at all, so you've doubled my assistance. I'll be fine."

I wasn't going to tell Chava that usually I didn't do this kind of thing at all, but I figured that wouldn't build her confidence in me.

Or build mine in myself, for that matter.

When she started to speak again, I pulled her close in a hug. I don't know which one of us was more surprised by my action, but I will say, it did shut her up.

"Keep the phone charging," I said, plugging it back in and setting it on the dash. "It's right here if you need it. See you soon."

With that, I climbed out of the car and closed the door behind me. The soft clunk sounded loud to my ear, though no one was around to hear it anyway. Without looking back, I struck off to my left, staying in the shadows until I could no longer see the front of the warehouses. Then I crossed the street and tucked up against the fence. I carefully worked my way around the south end to the far side of Leeds's property, away from any street traffic that might appear, even this early in the morning. A few minutes later, I reached the water side of the warehouses, the fence line strung out along the lip of the concrete slab that ended at the edge of the bay.

From my new vantage point, I could see the lot in back of the warehouses also sat empty, with no cars anywhere in sight. The lighting on the front of the main building didn't continue around the side or back, leaving the rest of the buildings without illumination.

I'd kept my eyes peeled for any kind of break in the fence, hoping there would be a place I could worm my way through. I wasn't keen on trying to scale the chain link that towered over my head, especially given the concertina wire spiraled around the top, waiting to rip a trespasser to shreds.

Scanning the backside of the fence, I found what I was looking for. The good news was a section of the chain link was missing. The bad news was it was on the side facing the bay, so I was going to have to hang out over the water and climb across to where I could get through the gap. The most difficult part would be swinging around the corner of the fence where it made a 90-degree turn out over the water. A section of fence was missing there too; however, the concrete slab had also fallen away, so I couldn't crawl underneath to the other side. I could reach a portion of fence still intact, but what I needed was something to help me swing through the missing section. Removing my gun from the holster and tucking it into my pants, I set the holster on the ground where I could pick it up on my return trip. Stretching out as far as I could reach, I threaded my belt through the chain link and buckled it, making a giant loop.

Swinging like Tarzan, or rather, Jane, I flew around the missing fence and caught my toes on the miniscule concrete ledge on the other side. Without stopping to think too much about the frigid water underneath me, I grabbed the chain link and secured my hold before dropping my makeshift trapeze.

Slowly, inch by inch, I worked my toes into the diamond shapes of the chain link to monkey my way the twenty or so feet to the space in the fence. My fingers felt like they might get ripped off my hands and my toes felt compressed into bricks by the time I reached the gap. Pulling myself through the hole, I started toward the largest warehouse, hoping after my physical antics I'd found the place Leeds had Kendra detained. The other buildings were mere skeletons, with large open gaps in doors or walls, so I guessed he'd have her stashed in the central warehouse, which remained the most complete.

I got to the back of the building without tripping and breaking an ankle on the uneven concrete in the dark, so I felt pretty good as I arrived at the back door. This one had a much more secure set of locks on it than Leeds's house, including a chain and padlock, a door lock, and a few deadbolts. It also had a few fifty-five gallon drums standing against the back wall, underneath a clerestory window. I climbed up on top one of them, giving me just enough height to peer inside.

It was pitch dark. No lights on, nothing to help me. I waited, hoping my eyes would adjust even a little to the faint moonlight and low sodium glow from the light at the front, which proved to be all the light I was going to get.

After what felt like hours but was probably only minutes, I could make out basic shapes inside the building. Large I-beams held up the ceiling. Giant metal racks and shelving units spread out around the walls and across the floor. White streaks covered everything, and I could hear the gentle cooing of pigeons tucked in for the night inside their abandoned urban dwelling.

Nothing moved below me. I carefully shined my flashlight through the window and checked out the room. At the far end to my left, I could see one interior door. The only other doors I could see in the whole place had images of stick figures—one male, one female.

I didn't think there was any power on in the building, so I didn't anticipate an alarm, but the locks were going to be a test of my skills. I didn't see any other way in, however. The broken windows were high enough to be a challenge to climb through, and I didn't see anything on the inside that would help me climb back out. The last thing I wanted was to get myself stuck inside with no cell, especially not knowing what kind of condition Kendra might be in.

Ten minutes later I had the padlock and chain off and the two deadbolts undone. I just had the lock in the door handle left to pick. My hands were cold, and I took a break between each lock to warm my fingers up before I tackled the next one. I guessed the temperature hovered right around twenty degrees, with the occasional gust of wind dropping it lower, making my task very uncomfortable.

I clenched my teeth around the penlight, my breath visible in the cold, and started on the final lock. The satisfying *click* confirmed my success.

I pushed open the door, bracing myself against the screech of an alarm, but heard nothing except blessed silence. Stepping into the warehouse, I pulled the door closed behind me and waited again for anything that would make me regret my plan of action. Visions of Doberman pinschers racing over to pounce on me danced through my head, but I appeared to have the warehouse to myself.

Clicking my flashlight on again to avoid falling over objects on the floor, I made my way over to the only door I could see that wasn't a restroom. Kendra would have said if she was locked in a bathroom. Arriving there in one piece, I crouched down to put my ear against the wood and heard the faint sound of movement. Was it Kendra or someone else? Someone else who wouldn't be quite so happy to see me.

I looked around for something to throw and finally found an abandoned ceramic coffee cup left behind by one of the former inhabitants. Hunched down behind a metal rack, I pulled my gun out in one hand and hurled the cup against the door with the other. The cup smashed gloriously against the solid wood door, but nothing happened. No one came out to investigate the source of the noise.

After a few minutes, I crossed back over to the door and crouched down to look at the lock. One more round with the lock picks and I had the door open—nothing but more darkness. I heard movement, but from what I couldn't tell.

Shining my light around, I discovered Kendra, trussed and tied up and lying on a sofa, duct tape over her mouth. She lay under an old sleeping bag but was still shivering in the cold. I gave the small room a quick once over. No one else sat waiting for me in the dark, so I shoved my gun into the back of my waistband and rushed over to free Kendra.

After I ripped the duct tape off her mouth, she let out a hoarse cry. "That hurt," she said.

"You're welcome. Where's Leeds?"

"I thought he went looking for you."

"What are you talking about?"

"When he came in, he discovered I'd lifted his cellphone and made that call to you. That's when he tied me up and duct-taped my mouth. Careful!" she said as I pulled out the Swiss army knife to cut the Zip Ties he'd used to bind her hands and feet.

"Why would he go looking for me? And why leave you here?"

"He didn't think you'd find me. How did you, by the way?"

"Never mind that now. What was he going to do to me?"

"I told him I didn't make any calls at all, that the battery died. But of course he just plugged it into a charger in his car and found your number. So I told him I got your voicemail and didn't have time to leave a message before the battery failed. When he saw my call lasted less than a minute, he thought that might be true, but he didn't want to take a chance. He was going to go over to your place and see if you were still there sleeping or if you had called the police or something."

"This doesn't make any sense. Why leave you here? Why not stuff you in the trunk again and take you with him?"

By this time I'd gotten her hands and feet unbound and was rubbing her extremities to get the blood going.

"Can you stand?" I asked. "Let's just get out of here and you can explain it all later."

Kendra stood, grimacing from the pain of pins and needles as the blood started circulating again.

"I'm all right," she said, starting to limp toward the door. "Let's go."

We went out the way I came in, Kendra complaining loudly about climbing through the fence.

"What if I fall in the water?" she'd said.

"I can leave you here instead. The back door to the warehouse is still open; you can just wait for Leeds to come back."

That shut her up, and she managed to climb the distance around the end of the fence onto solid ground, even navigating the place where my belt was the only handhold. Then it was my turn. I'd done this once before with no problem. I could do it again, right?

The wind picked up as I reached the gap where my belt hung. I stopped for a moment, waiting for the gust to settle. Looking down, all I could see was the black expanse of water several feet below.

Don't look down, I told myself. Trust that you can do this. There's nothing terrifying below you. I leapt.

Just as I started to swing across the opening, the wind returned with a vengeance. The power of it shook the chain link, pushing the water against the pilings beneath me and twisting me away from the fence.

The falling took me by surprise, but not as much as the sharp pain of the cold water hitting my face or the panic that overtook me as I could feel myself start to sink.

Chapter Twenty-Five

---•---

UTTER BLACKNESS SURROUNDED ME. My clothing was weighed down with water, my boots were heavy, and my jacket clutched my arms like a jilted lover refusing to let go. I'd managed a gulp of air before my head went under, but that wouldn't last long.

"Boots first," I heard Coop's voice in my head.

I struggled to pull them off, grateful they had quick laces on them and I wasn't dealing with knots. I tried not to think about how far I'd sunk when I finally started to push myself toward the surface. Breaking through to the cold, night air, I managed to gasp in a few breaths before the weight of my sodden clothes pulled me down again.

"Get that coat off," Coop's voice came again.

Thankful I'd left it unzipped, I shrugged and gyrated underwater to take it off. Just when I thought my lungs would burst, I freed myself of my winter coat and shot back up to the surface. Treading water, I frantically looked around for a way out. I'd drifted a little farther out in my struggles. I could see a small section of open sandy beach off to my right and started swimming that direction. My limbs were going numb, and the surface of the water got rougher as the wind continued to rise. Despite the fact it wasn't far away, I started to wonder if I'd make it before hypothermia set in and I sank like a stone. Kendra was unlikely to be of any use, and Chava wouldn't even know I was in trouble. A wave came from behind me and crashed over my head, pushing me back under again.

Fighting my way back up, I thought I'd never get to the surface, but just when I thought it was too hard, I felt something clamp down on the back of my shirt and begin to pull. Had Kendra jumped in to save me? That felt very out of character. I couldn't picture Chava leaping in to save me either, but maybe I was in for a surprise. There had been a lot of that lately.

Regardless of who my heroine was, it worked, and I broke the surface. With my guardian angel pushing and pulling from behind, I surged toward the shore with a final burst of energy. I could feel the bottom of the bay slam into my feet, and I crawled out of the water gasping for breath just as my savior crawled out behind me. Turning to thank whomever it was, I came face to face with a most peculiar person I'd ever met.

For a moment I thought Lonnie the Enforcer had magically appeared on the scene. This guy's face was even hairier, his gray moustache dripping water down his long nose. His eyebrows shadowed big dark eyes, his tongue hanging out between big white teeth.

I'd been helped by a dog.

The biggest, weirdest-looking bundle of ragged fur I'd ever seen. He stood a moment on the shore before shaking out his long tresses with such violence I thought for a moment he was having a seizure.

"Eddie! Are you okay?" I heard Kendra's voice come from the parking lot above me. "Can you hear me?"

I waved up at her, unable to speak, my teeth were chattering so hard. Knowing I could still die from shock and exposure in the cold, I pushed myself up to standing and started making my way up the bank to where Kendra stood.

"Oh, my god, oh my god, oh my god," Kendra chanted her mantra as I stumbled up next to her. "You fell in!"

I nodded and looked around. The dog scrambled up behind me and stood, nearly to my waist, as if waiting for a command.

"G-g-g-good boy," I stuttered out between frozen lips.

"We've got to get you warm," Kendra said, once more stating the obvious. "You're going to freeze to death."

I nodded and started moving, my feet too numb to feel the pebbles and rocks I'm sure I was walking across. The three of us made our way to my car, where I expected Chava to pop out to help—at least to dry me off and criticize me for falling in.

But she didn't pop out, because she was gone.

Chapter Twenty-Six

———•———

I LOOKED AROUND, HOPING CHAVA had gotten out to pee in the relative privacy of the darkness.

"Chava!" I called. "Where are you?"

"What are you doing?" Kendra asked. "Start the car up. Get the heater going."

That was the smartest thing I'd ever heard her say. Struggling into the car, I was relieved to see the keys were still in the ignition. I started up the engine and cranked the heater, my entire body quaking with the cold. I looked up and saw the big dog looking at me from just outside the door, his height making us eye level.

I got out of the car and opened the back door, immediately the mass of wet, dirty dog filled the entire bench seat.

"You can't let that mutt in here," Kendra said. The fact the dog was currently more help than she was had apparently escaped her attention. "He stinks!" she continued as I returned to the front seat, waiting for the heat to thaw me out enough to look for Chava.

"Let's get out of here," Kendra said, leaving the dog issue behind. "Do you want me to drive?"

"We can't leave yet. My mother is missing."

"Your mother?"

"She was in the car, waiting for me. Now she's gone."

"Gone where? There's nowhere to go."

Had she gone looking for me? Maybe she was out on the other side of Leeds's building, thinking she could see something. Had she fallen in the dark and turned an ankle? Or fallen into the water herself? I half expected her to come limping up at any moment. My cellphone sat on the dash where I'd left it. I picked it up and found a text.

I have something you want. You have something I want.

I could feel the blood draining from my face. I'd always thought that was just an expression, but I could actually feel my face go cold again, despite the heater turned on high and blowing right at me. Anxiety clenched my gut, like an unexpected fist in a bar fight, deep and visceral. I went to see who the text came from, but realized it had been typed into my phone, not sent from another.

"Shit," I said, pounding on my steering wheel.

"What? What is it?"

"He's got my mother. Where would your buddy Leeds go?"

"What do you mean he's got your mother?"

"I don't understand this," I said under my breath. "What have I got that he wants?"

"What he wants?" Kendra said, something in her voice prompting me to turn and look at her.

"He says I've got something he wants. That can't be you. He had you; he's after something else."

"What makes you think it's Leeds?" Kendra said, not quite meeting my eye. "You must meet a lot of unsavory characters in your line of work."

"Right. And they're all hanging around out here in the middle of the night," I said, fear bringing my sarcasm out. "He must have been waiting to see if I showed up. Or followed me. Something. But why not just grab me? Why grab my mother?"

I sat for a moment hearing nothing but the sound of my own breathing, loud in my ear as I fought to catch my breath, followed by a low whine from the backseat.

The phone rang. The incoming number came up as restricted.

"Hello," I said after the second ring.

"I'm so sorry, Eddie," I heard Chava say before another voice came on the line.

"That's enough for now," a voice said. "Did you get my message?" The voice sounded odd, high pitched. I wondered if he was doing something to make it unrecognizable.

"I got it. What is it you think I have?"

"Not *think*, know. I know you have it."

Listening for any clues as to where my mother might be, I strained to hear background noise, but only the man's heavy breathing came through the phone.

"Well?" the voice said. Apparently I was supposed to 'fess up.

"I'm not really in the mood for guessing games," I said and hung up the phone.

"What are you doing?" Kendra asked. "Was that him? You hung up! Are you crazy? Do you know what kind of man you're dealing with?"

So much for it not being Leeds.

"I'm guessing he's a stone cold psychopath," I replied. A memory floated in my consciousness. Something I remembered doing when I was a kid. Chava and I had worked out a code system when we wanted to have a conversation in public no one else could understand. We'd gotten very good at understanding each other's clues. I desperately hoped she would remember. Digging through my glove box, I shoved aside Kendra's pouch of cash and pulled out my notebook and a pen. I wanted to be ready the next time he called. I rolled up my sleeve to keep from getting the paper wet. I was going to have to do something about my wet clothes or I wouldn't be of use to anyone.

"But why did you hang up on him?"

"Because if it's true I've got something he wants, he'll call back. I want him off his game."

The phone rang. "I wouldn't do that again," the voice said, and I could hear anger this time, not just the cold reserve from the first call. I hung up.

"Why are you pissing him off?" Kendra asked.

"I want him reacting, not just planning. He might make a mistake."

It might not be the smartest plan, but it was all I had.

The phone rang a third time. I put it on speaker and spoke first. "Put my mother back on or I keep hanging up on you. I need to know she's all right."

After a pause, I heard the phone being shuffled around and Chava's voice came on.

"Edwina?" I heard her say. She had to be rattled to revert back to Edwina.

"How you be, Chava?" I asked. It was our signal the game had started.

I heard a slight catch in her breath that made me think she understood.

"I be good, how's you?"

I gave her a silent cheer.

"Are you all right?"

I could almost hear the wheels turning in her mind as she tried to figure out how to give me the most information she could in our code.

"It's arid here and I'm cold, but other than that I'm okay, I'll probably be up all night."

I wrote down her words, wanting to get as much as I could. I'd sort out the meaning later.

"Are you hurt?"

"I had a nice ride in the front seat; it felt like an hour. Not as good as public transportation, but it didn't cost me a quarter."

"Okay, that's enough," the man's shrill voice broke through as I heard him snatch the phone back from Chava.

"How can I give you what I want if I don't know what it is?" I asked.

"Be at your house in half an hour."

He knew where I lived?

"If I see the police," the shrill voice continued, "your mom is dead. If you don't show, she's dead. If I hear you're doing anything I don't like, she's dead."

With that he hung up the phone.

I looked down at the sentences I'd written out.

"What are you doing?" Kendra asked. "How does that nonsense tell you anything?"

I explained to her the game Chava and I used to play.

"So what does your code tell you this means?"

"I'm not sure yet. It's mostly about opposites. For example, she says it's arid and she's cold. That means she's somewhere wet and hot."

"Wet and hot? In Bellingham? In the winter? That doesn't make sense."

"It's not literal. It could mean she's near water or on Bay Street."

"So basically it could mean anything. That's not a very good code."

Ignoring Kendra's critique, I continued, "Nice ride in the front seat. I'm going to guess that means she was stuffed in the trunk just like you were. Felt like an hour, but it didn't cost a quarter. Okay, it wasn't an hour—it didn't take me that long to get to you—so that much is clear. It didn't cost a quarter—"

"Twenty-five cents?" Kendra said. "Does that mean twenty-five minutes?"

"A quarter of an hour is fifteen minutes. She was in the car for fifteen minutes."

"What about 'not as good as public transportation'?" Kendra leaned over my shoulder.

"It could just be my mother reminding me she hates to take the bus, but I think what it really means is she's alone, or rather he's alone. So there's no one else there."

"How does any of this help you find her?"

"I don't know yet," I said as I pulled out the files I'd stolen from Leeds's apartment. I started thumbing through the properties again, hoping something would raise a red flag. Fifteen minutes later I was out of time and ideas.

"What now?" Kendra asked.

"Now we meet your buddy Leeds and see what shakes out."

Though I'd warmed up with the heater, I still wore soaking wet clothes and no shoes. I looked in the back of my car in hopes of finding my gym bag or at least an extra jacket or a towel. I came up with a pair of shorts, a stained t-shirt I used to wipe oil off my dipstick when checking the level, a pair of shower shoes, and a beach towel. I used the towel to get as dry as I could and put on the clothes. At least the shorts had an actual waistband, and I could tuck my gun in without it slipping out. I looked ridiculous and it wasn't going to help much against the cold, but at least I would be dry.

Opening the back door, I looked down at the wet dog. He was huge and I wasn't sure how excited he was going to be to get toweled off by a stranger. He'd saved my life, however, so I figured I owed him something.

"Nice doggy," I said as I gently reached in to dry him off. He whined once but lay still under my ministrations. I ended by putting the towel over his back like a blanket and got back into the car for the drive home. One way or another, I had to face the man who'd abducted Kendra, snatched my mother, and possibly killed Deirdre Fox.

At least for now we were all alive. I just had to hope I could keep us that way.

Chapter Twenty-Seven

---·---

W E ARRIVED AT MY HOUSE just after six in the morning. With almost two hours to go before dawn, the streets were still dark, though traffic had increased. Pulling up half a block from my place, I looked around. I didn't see any cars parked nearby I didn't recognize, and definitely no silver Lexus. My neighborhood was quiet and my own house was dark. Had Leeds returned the favor and broken in? Was he already waiting there for me?

Nothing to be done about it. I had to meet him to find Chava.

Kendra didn't want to come in with me and she also didn't want to wait in the car with the hulking canine in the backseat; besides, Leeds might see her. She didn't want to go home—though I had no time to take her out there in any case. I wasn't sure what I was going to do with her.

"There's a coffee shop a few blocks back," she said, referencing a small place already open for the early morning crowd.

"Are you sure?" I asked, thinking she'd probably bolt as soon as I dropped her off.

"What else am I going to do?" she asked. "I'm not safe either until you stop him."

Not having any better ideas, short of stuffing her in the trunk, which my Subaru doesn't have, I agreed and turned around to drop her off.

I watched her go inside and returned to my home, which felt a lot less safe than it had yesterday.

I unlocked the front door and left it that way. There was no use lying in wait to jump the guy. I needed him to tell me where Chava was. I had to hope there would be some honor among thieves and we'd both figure out a way to get what we wanted.

Pulling my gun out, I wanted to make sure I'd drained residual water out of the barrel. I knew a gun could still fire after being submerged, but water left behind could act like an obstruction, and water didn't compress. No water came out and I checked the cylinders. It all looked good. Before I could do anything further, even change my clothes, I heard the front door open. I shoved the gun back in my waistband, pulled the t-shirt down, and looked up to see a man I didn't recognize. No taller than me, he was built like someone used to physical labor, thick arms and thighs. A scar under his right eye gave him a dangerous air, even before I saw the rather large gun in his hand.

"Christopher Leeds, I presume?" I said as he came inside.

"Hello, Ms. Shoes," he said. His voice really did squeak; he hadn't been masking it on the phone. The high-pitched sound did not match his bulky frame. No wonder he'd muffled it when he answered Kendra's phone a few nights ago; it was very distinctive. I would have laughed at him if he wasn't holding Chava's life in his hands.

"Come on in and sit yourself down. Tell me what I can do for you," I said.

Leeds came forward and sat in a chair across from the sofa. "Does this mean you're going to be reasonable?

"I'm always reasonable," I said. "Where's my mother?"

"She's safe, for now. An ... acquaintance of mine is staying with her. You do what I want, and I will call and tell him not to put a bullet in her head."

"So what is it you want from me?"

"Kendra gave you a little something for safekeeping. I want it back."

"Kendra never gave me anything."

"Yes, she did."

"Why are you so sure of this?"

"She told me."

"In case you haven't noticed, Kendra lies," I said. "She'd tell you anything you wanted to hear, especially if you held a gun to her head."

"I think I know Kendra a little better than you do," Leeds said. "I know her tells when she's lying. She's got one I can see a mile away."

"What is your history with Kendra?" I asked. Curiosity always did get the better of me.

"She hasn't given you the whole story?" Leeds finally relaxed his hand on the gun. "Kendra and I go way back. She and I are—"

At just that moment, the very woman we were talking about walked in through my front door. Her gun was smaller than either one of ours, but it looked just as deadly.

Apparently Mr. Leeds didn't know Kendra as well as he thought he did. Unless, of course, she brought the gun to use on me, and that had been the plan all along.

Chapter Twenty-Eight

———·———

A FTER A VERY LONG MOMENT of silence, Kendra stepped a little farther into the room, her gun pointed squarely at Leeds.

"Hello, Karl," Kendra said. "Surprised to see me?"

Karl?

"A little. I figured you'd have bolted again."

Again?

"I'm done running from you. I want to get you out of my life for good."

"Are you sure, Kendra? You jumped at the chance to work with me again."

There was that pesky "again" again. What exactly was the history between these two?

"That was before I knew you killed Deirdre."

"I thought you didn't like Deirdre."

"It doesn't matter if I liked her or not; it's about you crossing a line."

"How about I just go pick up my mother from wherever you have her stashed and the two of you can hash this out," I said, breaking into their touching little reunion. "You can even stay here and use my house for as long as you want."

The two looked at me, Karl with a glare and Kendra as if she'd forgotten I was there.

"Maybe we should all just put the guns away?" I said, my hand resting on my own gun nestled at the small of my back. "We don't want anyone doing anything foolish by mistake, do we?" I used my quietest, calmest voice, as if I were talking to baby animals lost in the woods. "Everybody wants something here. Let's just sit down, talk this through and see if we can arrive at a solution that makes everybody happy."

I could see a little nonverbal communication spin out between the two. Clearly they had a lot of history. Much as I worried about Chava, the dynamic here was fascinating

It was an occupational hazard.

Moving away from each other, the two gun-toting miscreants sat down in the chairs that faced my sofa, though neither one put their gun away. With Kendra's gun on Karl and Karl's gun on me, I felt like I was in the middle of a scene from the movie *Reservoir Dogs*. Quentin Tarantino would have loved these two.

"There, that's better. Why don't we start with you, Kendra, since *Karl* here doesn't want to tell me what it is he thinks I have." I wasn't going to start asking about why Christopher Leeds was suddenly going by Karl, but if they wanted to fill in the blanks, fine by me.

"I want Karl to leave me alone."

Coming after him with a gun didn't seem like the right way to make that happen, but being new to this situation, I decided to keep my mouth shut.

"Why would you want that?" Karl said. And I noticed his attention on Kendra meant his gun was pointed just a little less toward me.

"Why? Because you're a bully, Karl Turner. You've been a bully for almost my entire life. I'm done with it. I'm done with the life of a con artist. I just wanted a normal life, with a good man, and you ruined that."

Wait, what? Life of a con artist? The clouds parted and I understood a lot more than I had before this conversation started.

"Let me get this straight," I said, even knowing Karl's gun would get pointed back at me. "You two have worked together before? This is what you do? Your marriage to Hallings ... that was just a scam?"

Kendra started to cry, her gun hand quivering enough to make me even more nervous.

"No! That's the problem. It wasn't a scam. I'd turned my life around. I ran away from Karl almost three years ago, but he found me. He tracked me down ... again."

"Why not just let her go?" I asked Karl.

"Because I love her," the man said. "I would have come for her sooner, except I was ... detained."

I almost believed him.

Kendra's tears continued to fall, her sobs causing her gun to veer wildly around the room.

"Kendra," I said, "I need you to pull it together for me."

"I'll ..."—sob—"I'll ..."—sob—"try." Sob.

She did, however, get a grip on her weapon. Where the hell had that thing come from anyway? Something else I'd have to ask about if I didn't die in the next hour.

Much as I didn't want to play marriage counselor between two felons, my goal was to keep my mother alive, so I thought I'd better give it a shot.

"Karl," I said, "if Kendra wants to be left alone, maybe you should honor that. She might come back to you on her own."

The softer side of the man of steel disappeared again in an instant. His laugh sent shivers down my spine, and not in a good way.

"This is where you tell me if you love something set it free, right? And if it loves you, it will come back, and if it doesn't, let it go?"

The thought had crossed my mind.

"Well, I've got a different version of that story."

Having read my fair share of bumper stickers, I knew what was coming next.

"If it doesn't come back, hunt it down and shoot it."

Karl swung his gun away from me and pointed it toward Kendra. I was slightly relieved to no longer be in the line of fire from either one of them, but a shoot-out in my living room wasn't going to help me find Chava. I toyed with the idea it would save me a lot of hassle if they just injured each other enough to incapacitate themselves, but given the likelihood they'd both die and I'd be tied up with the police all day, I decided it wasn't worth it.

"Karl, you don't want to kill Kendra. If you did, wouldn't you have already done it?"

"I've got a lot of time and money invested in this girl. She doesn't get to just walk away."

I kept my eyes on Kendra. If she planned to off Karl, she'd kill the only link to my mother.

"Why didn't you kill me when you had the chance?" Kendra asked.

"I figured when you calmed down, you'd see this is for the best. After all, you hitched your wagon to that Hallings guy, thinking that would save you, and he turns out to be a cheating loser and broke to boot. Not much of a white knight."

"He's a cheating loser because you set him up!"

"No. He cheated because I gave him the chance and he took it. The loser part he did all on his own. He's broke, sweetheart. And he's in trouble with the Mafia. Don't tell me you're going to stand by your man after he slept with Deirdre and he's got nothing in his bank account."

"That's none of your business."

"It is exactly my business. Our business, if I can remind you. You were all ready to come back to me."

"When I thought my husband cheated on me!"

"He did cheat on you."

"He never would have done that if you hadn't sicced Deirdre on him. I didn't know you'd set him up when I agreed to go after the divorce."

"It didn't take much to get you to turn on him," Karl said, and I had to admit, he had a point.

I must have made some kind of noise because Kendra turned to me.

"You've got to believe me, Eddie. I was going to take the money from the divorce and disappear again. I wanted to get away from Karl and I thought my husband killed Deirdre. It was just too much to take."

Then she learned he was broke. I wondered which of these little events bothered her the most.

Parsing through Kendra's pack of lies, I sorted out what truth might lay in her words.

"You know what you are, Kendra," Karl said, his voice oily but somehow compelling. "You're the best scam artist I've ever seen. You love the art of the game. Identifying the mark, setting the trap, lying in wait. It's what you do. It's what *we* do. I'll bet you've been bored to tears married to a car salesman. Don't tell me you haven't missed me just a little bit."

He had a point there too. After all, she could have paid me easily, but she scammed me just because she could.

"You don't know me at all," Kendra said.

And then she shot him.

Chapter Twenty-Nine

———•———

I'M NOT SURE WHICH OF US was the most surprised by Kendra's actions. And that included Kendra. The pop from the tiny gun didn't sound like it had actually fired. Karl made more noise than the gun itself. He grunted and grabbed at his side, where a blossom of bright red blood appeared under his fingers.

"What the hell is that thing," Karl asked, making me think his wound would not be immediately fatal.

"An MSP Silent Pistol," Kendra said, her tears temporarily dry and her hands much steadier than before.

"I need to get one of those," he said before slumping over further and gripping his side tighter.

I walked over to Karl and saw him raise his gun to point at me again.

"Oh, give it a rest, Karl. Do you want to bleed to death on my floor? Kendra just changed the rules of the game."

"I've still got your mother," he said.

"Why do you think I don't want you to die?" I asked as I pushed his gun to the side, though he tightened his grip on it as I ripped his shirt open. I'd always wanted to do that to a man, but this wasn't how I imagined it would go.

The bullet had dug a gouge through his body at the bottom of his rib cage. I had the urge to poke him and ask if it hurt, but I still needed him.

"Did it go all the way through?" Kendra asked, wonder in her voice.

I pulled Karl forward. He made a loud "oooouuufffing" sound and I found a hole in the back of his shirt.

"It looks superficial," I said, assessing the hole in my chair. I didn't see an exit hole to match, so Kendra's bullet appeared to be stuck inside.

"Did I kill him?"

"Not even close," Karl said, though his skin had gone a little gray and he'd started to sweat.

"Maybe not, but you don't look so good," I said, leaning him back in the chair.

"You've got to help me or you'll never see your mother again."

"Let him bleed to death," Kendra said, rising out of her chair. I had a moment of fear she planned to shoot him again.

"Will both of you shut up?" I said. "Kendra. You do not want to kill this man. He's not worth it. Right now you've just shot in self-defense. Let's not make this any worse. Karl, just tell me where my mother is and I'll get you medical attention."

This may have sounded cold—whether or not he held my mother hostage—but I didn't think the bullet had done any real damage. He wasn't even bleeding that much, though shock might be a problem.

Besides, I'd survived falling into freezing cold water, late at night, in the middle of winter. Surely this Karl person could handle a tiny gunshot wound.

Karl leaned back again, and I could see his fingers relax on the gun. I reached out and grabbed it as fast as I could, wrenching it out of his hand before he could fire.

"Goddamn it," he said, his breath coming fast and heavy.

I checked the safety and shoved his gun in my pocket—

which was very awkward, but I didn't want it anywhere Kendra could grab it—and pulled him out of the chair and onto the floor.

"What are you doing?" Kendra asked.

"I'm going to bandage up his wound and go find my mother."

"Well, I'm not going to help you now," Karl said. I fought the urge to kick him.

I went into my kitchen and grabbed a clean dish towel and a roll of duct tape out of the junk drawer.

"Help me," I said to Kendra, who still looked a bit dazed.

"Why?"

"Because if you don't I'm going to turn you in."

"I've got a gun," she said, turning her little weapon on me.

I pulled my own gun out of my waistband and simultaneously pulled Karl's back out of my pocket.

"I've got two," I said, pointing them at her pretty face. "More importantly, I've got at least fifty pounds on you and extensive training in martial arts, so I can kick your ass without the firepower. You aren't going to shoot me, but I don't need you to get my mother back, so I might just shoot you to get you out of my way."

"You wouldn't," she said.

"Try me. I have officially reached the end of my rope."

My hands definitely didn't shake as I pointed both guns in her direction. Standing only a couple feet away, she was looking down the barrels of two very deadly weapons.

"I could use a little help here," Karl said.

"Fine, what do you want me to do?" Kendra stuffed her tiny, quiet gun back into whatever little pocket she'd hidden it in.

My precious, I thought to myself, complete with Gollum voice. I'd have to get the gun away from her at some point. For a first-time shooter, she seemed to have enjoyed it a little too much.

At least I hoped it had been a first.

Directing Kendra, I got Karl bandaged up and rolled him

onto his back on the floor. I thought about putting his feet up on the coffee table, remembering something about keeping blood flow to a person's head, but I wasn't sure if that was the right move for this type of problem, so I just left him lying there.

"Now what?" Kendra asked.

Now that I knew he wasn't going to bleed to death in my house, I sat back on my heels and contemplated the situation. The way I saw it, I had a couple of options. I could bring the police in at this point. Apparently I had Deirdre's killer and his accomplice. The cops would have to listen to me. The other option was to torture Karl a little bit and see if he'd cough up my mother's whereabouts. But which of those would be the most productive? Karl chose that moment to open his mouth and make the decision for me.

"She's running out of time," he said. And I knew he wasn't talking about Kendra.

Chapter Thirty

———•———

"**W**HAT THE HELL DOES THAT mean?" I asked. "Running out of time how?"

The man laughed, or at least that's what it sounded like, as it ended in a groan.

"Where. Is. She?" I leaned in over Karl's face, so he could see the dangerous glint in my eye, and at least one of the guns I was holding.

Apparently the glint didn't look all that dangerous because he just smiled back at me.

That's when I leaned my knee into the neatly bandaged gunshot wound.

He cried out, probably as much from surprise as from pain.

"Where. Is. My. Mother," I said, easing up a little bit.

"I've still got the better hand, here," Karl said. "You need me to find her, and I can guarantee she'll be dead soon if I don't make a phone call. Play ball with me or you become an instant orphan."

Now didn't seem to be the time to let him know I would actually have one parent left, who was apparently a contract killer for the Mafia. I couldn't see how to turn that to my advantage.

Instead, I started to lean in again, using the barrel of Karl's gun pressed against the exact spot the bullet ripped through his side, but before he said anything, Kendra finally became useful.

"I've got it! I've figured out the code!" she said, her excitement weirdly out of place, given the situation. She sounded more like a kid who'd just solved a particularly tough puzzle than an adult facing attempted murder and extortion charges.

"What?" I turned to look at her, my hand poised over Karl's wound, ready to poke it with his gun again.

"I know where he's got her. I know where your mother is."

THE FIRST QUESTION WAS WHAT to do with Karl. I knew he wouldn't die from blood loss, but shock could still become an issue. I didn't want to be a party to his murder, even if he was a monster. Spending the last couple years of my life chasing other people's demons had helped keep mine in check. Seeing the destruction other people wreaked helped me stay, if not honest, at least relatively ethical. And I especially didn't want him dying in my living room.

"Karl. Kendra and I are going to take a little drive. I think it would be in your best interest to come along."

"Why would I do that?" he asked.

"Would you rather stay here?"

His eyes shifted back and forth between Kendra and me. I could tell he was weighing his options. I figured, deep down, he still thought he could turn things around with her, even if she had shot him. She hadn't killed him after all. Maybe in their line of work a gunshot wound was a sign of affection.

"Fine," he said.

"Let's get him into the back of my car," I said, taking a page from his own playbook. I didn't have a trunk, but I could still fit him in the space between the backseat and the hatchback.

Karl started to argue when I opened up the back to help him in, but one look at the giant dog in the backseat and he curled himself up small enough to fit.

I took it for granted Kendra would go along with my plan, and it didn't occur to her she didn't have to. She seemed to be a woman used to taking orders, and while I might not typically reinforce that kind of behavior, for now I would use it to my advantage.

"This is for your own safety," I said as I duct-taped his hands and legs together. He might have tried to say something, but I slapped the tape over his mouth so I wouldn't hear it.

I covered him with the beach towel that had been on the dog and Kendra and I got into the front, where she could navigate me through the streets of Bellingham. Sunrise wouldn't be for another hour, so I wasn't worried about anyone seeing my strange cargo in the back.

The dog continued to lie quietly in the backseat. Once this was sorted out, I'd have to figure out what to do with him. He didn't have a collar on, but someone must be missing that enormous fuzzy face.

"Tell me about Karl's other partners in crime," I said, putting questions about the dog on a back burner. I also cranked up the heat again. I'd grabbed a coat out of the closet on the way out the door, but I was still dressed in shorts and shower shoes. I guess I wasn't thinking as clearly as I should be, knowing Chava was running out of time.

"I have no idea who it could be," Kendra replied, pointing to a street coming up. "Right turn there."

"Don't hold out on me now, Kendra," I said, taking the corner slow enough not to jostle Karl too badly or throw the dog to the floor.

"I'm serious, Eddie. Karl never worked with a partner, except me."

"And Deirdre," I said.

"Right. Her." I caught a glimpse of Kendra's face before she turned away, looking out the window.

"Jealous?"

"What? No. Why would you say that?"

"Something in your tone of voice just now."

Kendra didn't respond.

"Do you think he's lying?" I asked, shifting gears. "About someone holding a gun to my mother's head?"

"It's possible."

I was better off assuming there was someone else with my mother I'd have to disarm to get her safely away. I wished I wasn't going into this situation so blind. Maybe I'd get lucky and find Chava alone. We continued the rest of the trip in silence, each caught up with our own thoughts, broken only by Kendra's directions and the occasional grumble from the back of the car that could have been either Karl or the dog—I couldn't tell which.

"We're almost there," Kendra said after the last turn. "On the right."

Driving past the building Kendra pointed out, I turned around at the end of the next block and pulled up out of sight of anyone inside. I could see why Kendra thought of this place. It had been a coffee roaster in a previous life. Hot and wet would make sense in Chava's mind. And it definitely fit the "up all night" bit. The Sound Coffee Company's sign still hung above the door, but windows covered in brown paper showed it had been a long time since coffee beans were roasted behind these walls.

"I didn't see this listed in his properties," I said, eyeing the building through the trees that screened it from a distance.

"It's probably not listed by the coffee company," Kendra explained. "That was a renter; it would have been listed under retail."

"How did you know it was here?"

Kendra hesitated. My guess was telling me the truth would incriminate her in some way.

"Look, Kendra, I don't care what scams the two of you have

been involved with; I just want my mother safe. The more you can tell me, the better prepared I am when I storm that building. If she dies, you're guilty as an accomplice after the fact. Do you really want that hanging over your head?"

I gave her a moment to think about it. If I pushed her too hard I might get nothing useful.

"I went with Karl, after he moved here, to see what holdings Christopher Leeds had."

"Who is Christopher Leeds? Just a made-up name?"

"No. He's a real person. He doesn't live in the area so no one knows what he actually looks like. The real Christopher Leeds is ancient, and dying. Karl stole his identity, and then came out here and used it to make a little cash."

"How did he make money stealing the guy's identity?"

"Easy," Kendra said, shaking her head like anyone should see this. "Leeds had automatic deposits for most of his properties, so Karl just chose a few, which he contacted pretending to be Leeds with new account information. The renter doesn't have any reason to suspect it's someone else using Leeds's name, so they just change the account they deposit to."

"Doesn't Leeds notice he no longer has any money coming in from that renter?"

"He's so ill, probably not. Karl does his research. He sends a thirty-day notice to vacate to Leeds, along with another address to send the deposit back to, as if it's coming from the renter. So Leeds thinks the account is closed. Thirty days later, the renter sends the rent to the new bank account, which Karl set up, and the money is deposited there. He can usually keep a scam like that going for a couple months, and there's almost no way to trace him. He has the money immediately forwarded by wire into another bank account, owned by some shell company he's created. There are so many fake names on top of fake names it would take forever to track it all down. And you'd have to care enough to do it. Taken renter by renter, it's not much money, but adding it all together, it's a lot."

"How much income are we talking about?"

"Several thousand dollars a month." Kendra shrugged as if that meant little. "Commercial real estate is a mess right now. No one who holds as many properties as Leeds does would be too wound up about a few, smaller retail places in low-rent areas sitting empty. Even if he was healthy, it's doubtful he'd rush to fill the spaces. Karl keeps an eye on Leeds, in case he makes a move to look into anything, but with someone like Leeds it can go on even longer. He'll probably die soon and his estate will be in probate for months. Karl does his homework really well." There was a certain annoying pride in Kendra's voice. "He picked someone without a clear heir. The extended family will be fighting for years. No one will know what's rented to whom or who owns what."

"Jandyce versus Jandyce."

"What?"

"Dickens?"

Kendra continued to look blank.

"*Bleak House.* The endless lawsuit where no one makes out except the barristers?"

"I have no idea what you're talking about."

I guessed Kendra's education didn't include a lot of English Literature.

"Did you see the inside?" I asked, giving up on the Charles Dickens reference.

"I did. It's still full of coffee roasting equipment and espresso machines, things like that. Another way the scam makes money is Karl sells anything of value left behind in a vacated property; he was thinking about liquidating out here."

"How does he get around not having the keys to any of these empty buildings?"

"Karl's got an entire locksmith operation set up in a van he keeps elsewhere. He just rekeys any property he needs to get into. When he's dressed in a locksmith uniform, no one thinks twice about it. He's not the type you notice. He's invisible.

People change locks on newly vacated businesses all the time."

Thousands of dollars a month? I was in the wrong business. I even had a head start since I owned those fancy lock picks of mine. Except, I wasn't a thief. Or a murderer. Burglar, yes, but I never actually took anything after I broke in. Well, except for Leeds's files. I guess I did technically steal those, except the circumstances were dire. I thought Kendra was being held against her will. And they weren't really Leeds's files, since Leeds was really Karl Turner, who was a criminal, right?

Pushing thoughts of the ethical nature of my own behavior out of my head for now, I brought my attention back to where we thought Karl might have hidden my mother.

"Is there a back entrance?"

"Yes," Kendra said. "There's a back door, no windows, that leads out to the alley behind the building."

Kendra went on to describe as much of the layout of the inside as she could remember. Thinking about what she told me, I guessed Karl would have Chava in the back, in the storeroom. It would be the most secure part of the building, and no one would hear her from outside.

The question of the day, however, was whether or not Chava was in there alone. She might have been when they arrived, but someone else had been brought in after the phone call to me.

"You stay here," I said to Kendra as I got out of the car.

"Okay," she said meekly. "What if there's someone else in there, and he comes out and sees me?"

"Stay down," I said. "If I'm not back soon, call the police."

"I don't have a cell."

I debated giving her mine, but what if I needed it?

"There's a gas station a few miles back. Drive there if you have to and use the pay phone."

I popped open the hatch to take a quick look at Karl, who rolled his eyes at me and made whiny noises. I didn't really care what he had to say at this point, so I ignored him. At least he was still breathing and wasn't going to die from shock anytime soon. The giant, gray mass of fur sat up enough to look over the edge of the backseat at me, but he just plopped back down. I guess having a safe, dry car felt like heaven after being outside on the waterfront all night.

I left the keys in my ignition, hoping Kendra wouldn't just drive away as soon I disappeared from view. She was the only hope I had if things went sideways. I'd thought about waking Iz, then remembered she was spending a long weekend up in the San Juan Islands. The list of friends I could count on pretty sparse. I thought about Chance Parker too, but that would be even more complicated. Plus, he'd do everything by the book and for me Chava's safety came first, meaning we could end up wanting different things.

If I survived the night, maybe I should think about finding a few more friends.

Moving through the trees, I came up on the building from the west side. With only a few windows high up, I wouldn't be seen by anyone inside. I crept around back and surveyed the door. It was just as Kendra described it: two dumpsters sat not far away—one for garbage, one for recycling. There were no windows, only a single door to the right and a rolling door to the left.

I considered sneaking around to the front of the building to peer through one of the covered windows. However, the chances were better that I would be seen by someone inside rather than actually doing myself any good.

I'd just have to go through the back door and hope for the best.

At the back door, I studied the locks. Luckily they didn't pose any serious challenge, and I had them picked and open in less than a minute. I held my breath as I slowly opened the door a crack and peered inside.

The room was a dark cavern. Despite the sky growing light outside, it was even darker than the warehouse because there were fewer windows. Nothing stirred, and at least this time everything wasn't covered in pigeon droppings. I opened the door just wide enough to slide in and closed it behind me. Standing with my back to the door, I slowed my breathing and listened but heard nothing. The only thing to alert my senses was the smell of coffee beans. I pulled my gun and the extra penlight I'd retrieved from my glove box—my good one having sunk to the bottom of the bay along with my coat and Swiss army knife—and checked out the room I was in.

Large vats and shiny aluminum machinery filled the room. Clearly this was where the roasting was done, with the front area reserved for the coffee shop. The storeroom/office combination Kendra described would be in front of me to the right.

I made my way across roughly twenty feet of open floor without tripping and falling into a vat. The door didn't have a lock, but I placed my ear against it and listened again.

Still nothing.

Holding my breath, I edged the door open.

Still dead quiet.

Good news or bad?

Swinging the door open I thanked the hinge gods nothing squeaked or gave away my presence. It was so quiet. Was I even in the right place? Shining my flashlight around, I could see tall storage racks on either side of me.

Was Chava being held somewhere else?

Maybe Kendra had distracted me long enough to take off with Karl and my car. I stopped for a moment, frozen. Should I go back out and see if they were still there?

I'd come this far. I decided to commit and hope for the best. How far could Kendra get in a stolen car, a guy with a gunshot wound stashed in the back?

"And your dog," a little voice in my head said.

Where did that voice come from? He wasn't my dog. I'm not a dog person.

Was I?

Willing my feet to move, I shined my flashlight in front of me again. I could see another closed door at the far end. No light showed from underneath. If anyone occupied the room, they were sitting in the dark. Leaning against it, I caught the faint sound of movement.

Someone was on the other side.

The only thing I had going for me was surprise, so I decided to take my chances. I pushed the door open as fast as I could, pointing my gun in front of me and shining my light wildly around the room. It landed on my mother's face. Fear showed in her eyes, the whites wide and the pupils tiny. Her mouth covered with duct tape, she made noises as if she might be screaming behind the makeshift gag.

No one else inhabited the room with her, so maybe I had gotten lucky and Karl was lying about having a partner. Rushing to Chava's side, I went to pull the tape off and saw someone had placed handcuffs on her wrists and bound her legs with more duct tape.

I wish I'd paid a little more attention to Chava's expression, however, because I wouldn't have been quite so surprised when the lights burst on and a voice behind me told me to drop the gun.

I wasn't sure if the surprise was because someone else really was there, or because I recognized who it was even before I turned around.

Chapter Thirty-One

"HELLO, MR. HALLINGS," I SAID, as I greeted Chava's guard.

"You must be Eddie Shoes," he said, pointing yet another very large gun at my mother. "Nice of you to drop in."

What was it with everyone and their firepower? Way too many people had guns these days. I searched his face, trying to discern if he was the type capable of shooting another human being.

Having a gun and firing one were two very different things.

His face showed nothing, as if he'd buried his emotions some time ago and now relied solely on instinct. Not a good sign.

"I guess this really is a family affair," I said. "First Kendra, now you. Karl has you all under his thumb, doesn't he?"

"I'm not under anybody's thumb," Hallings said, though the tightness around his mouth indicated I'd hit a nerve.

"Is this how you're planning to get out of your debt to the Mob?"

Hallings eyes widened in surprise.

"Didn't think I knew about that, did you?"

"What's your point?"

"Well, I figure you're caught up in this because of your debt, but I'm also guessing you didn't have anything to do with killing Deirdre." I desperately hoped that was true and Karl really had killed her. "Which means, you could still walk away from this without making things worse."

"Is that so?" Hallings said, trying to sound tough, but I heard a note of desperation in his voice.

"Yep. Let my mother and me go and we'll forget we saw you here. Karl and Kendra were working together as far as I'm concerned."

"You're the least of my problems, Eddie," Hallings said. "Since you know about my debt and who I owe it to, I think you can understand that."

"Killing my mother isn't going to help your situation in any way," I said, thinking he might stop pointing his gun at her and point it toward me instead.

I didn't like seeing my defenseless mother restrained on the ground; him pointing a gun at her just made it worse.

"She's not going to be a moving target, so I think I'll keep my gun pointed at her."

"Okay, then. Why don't we just take a breath and talk this through," I said reasonably. "Maybe there's a way out for all of us."

It had worked on Karl and Kendra, or at least it had if you didn't count the part where she shot him.

"You want me to stay calm?" Hallings said. "Then go over and sit down next to Mommy Dearest."

I'd wanted to get closer to Chava anyway. I pretended to think about it before sighing and moving over to her. "You're the boss," I said, lowering my gun and kneeling down close to her.

Keeping my eyes on Hallings's gun, I reached out to Chava.

"How you doing?" I asked. Rubbing Chava's arm, I surreptitiously checked her pulse and respiration. Though clearly distressed at the situation, she didn't appear to be drugged or injured in any way. I could feel her tension ease just a fraction under my touch.

"So answer me this, Mr. Hallings," I said as I maneuvered myself into the best position. I knew I couldn't hold it forever, but for now I could stand up and throw myself at Hallings if I thought he was going to shoot. "Just how did this all come about? I don't understand how your affair with Deirdre was part of the scam."

"What scam?" Hallings said. "My affair with Deirdre was real."

"Real in the sense they were setting you up so Kendra could get half your estate?"

I could feel Chava pressing against my ankle, as if she wanted my attention. Looking down, I could see her eyes looking back and forth at the desk to our right, but for the life of me, I couldn't figure out why.

Hallings didn't reply, and I guessed I'd once again touched a nerve. I paused for a moment, weighing the options in front of me. I didn't know for sure if Kendra would contact the police if she heard shots or just make a run for the Canadian border in my car. Given her history, I had to assume the latter, which meant I was on my own here. I could shoot Hallings, but there was no guarantee he wouldn't get a shot off first, and if I was incapacitated and Chava was tied up, we could both die before anyone found us.

Negotiation might work, but I had to figure out what I had that Hallings might want. A way out with the Mob, maybe, but I didn't know how to deliver that. Maybe Chava did, though.

"I hear Vincent Careno is looking for you."

"That so?"

"I'll bet you didn't know my mother here is a friend of his."

"What are you talking about?"

"You don't know about my mother, do you, Mr. Hallings."

"What's there to know?"

"She's one of the finest poker players in Vegas."

"You're making that up. And why should I care?"

"Well. The road you're currently taking, if you don't end up locked up as accessory to murder, the Mob is going to kill you, right? Or make your life so miserable you'll wish you were dead."

Hallings didn't reply, leading me to believe I had his attention.

"Maybe there's another way out of this for you."

"And what would that be?"

"Chava here might be able to fix things for you with Vegas."

"Don't bullshit me," Hallings said. "I'm supposed to believe that woman there is some kind of card shark?"

"You don't have to believe me," I said, "Let me just take this gag off, and she can tell you herself." Without waiting for an answer, I leaned over and ripped the tape off Chava's mouth. She gasped from the sting of the tape but regained her voice.

"She's right," Chava managed to sputter out, sounding rough, but stronger than I thought she would be. "I've been playing in Careno's orbit for a lot of years now. I can make things right if you let us go."

"I'd have to be a first-class chump to buy that one. I just let you walk out of here and believe you're going to do that for me? I don't think so."

"I could set it up, right now, over the phone," Chava said.

She looked so serious even I believed her.

Hallings's expression changed for the first time since he'd turned the light on. I saw something there I didn't realize was missing until I saw it flash across his face.

Hope.

"What are you saying?"

"I'm saying …" Chava paused, with just a trace of annoyance in her voice, like she was talking to a truculent child instead of a grown man with a gun pointed in her face, "that I will call Vinnie right now and tell him I'm going to play on your behalf to settle your debt."

I thought the "Vinnie" was a nice touch.

"And why would *Vinnie* let you do that?" Hallings asked.

"Because he wants his money. He doesn't care how he gets it. He knows my skills. He's been wanting me to play for him for years. I go to work for him in exchange for dropping your debt."

She sounded so credible even I started to believe her. Maybe Chava wasn't kicked out of Vegas; maybe she was also running from the Mafia.

Or the law.

Regardless of how much truth she was telling, it seemed to be working on Hallings. Chava and I both saw his body posture shift from defiant to receptive. She was getting through to him.

"What exactly did Turner promise you?"

"Turner?"

"Leeds," I corrected, as Karl no doubt used his fake name with Hallings.

"He said if I stayed here and kept an eye on Mrs. Shoes here—"

"Schultz," Chava corrected.

I gave her a little kick in the shin.

"Schultz, whatever! Your mom here, he'd help me settle my debt with Careno."

"And how did he know about it to begin with?"

"I don't know."

"And that didn't worry you just a little? Especially after he killed your girlfriend?"

"He didn't kill Deirdre—Careno did—and now he's grabbed Kendra."

"Wait, what?"

"Careno, he's the one who's got Kendra."

"Uh, no he doesn't," I said.

"Yes, he does."

"I hate to argue with a man aiming a really big firearm at me and my mother, but no he doesn't."

"And just how do you know that?"

"Because Kendra is safe and sound and sitting in my car outside."

Now Hallings looked totally confused. His gun dipped just a little more. This guy was definitely an amateur.

"I don't believe you."

"Go outside and take a look."

"I'm not falling for that."

"I'm telling you the truth. Kendra's with me. How do you think I found this place? She told me about it. Karl, Leeds, whatever, had her stashed at a warehouse, but I went and got her out."

"That doesn't make any sense," Hallings said.

"Okay, let me see if I can straighten things out for you. Leeds came to you after Deirdre died and Kendra disappeared. He told you Careno did it and he would help you. Is that about right?"

"That's exactly right. He knew Careno was pressuring me to launder money through my dealership in exchange for dropping my debt. I didn't want to get trapped like that, but I couldn't pay him back either."

"Let me run another scenario past you. Deirdre, Kendra, and Leeds set you up. Kendra planned to divorce you, taking half your assets. Leeds killed Deirdre, then locked up Kendra after she got spooked by Deirdre's murder and decided to run. Then Leeds, trying to put a stop to all of this, talked you into this ridiculous Careno story to help him out. No doubt Leeds's eventual plan was to come here, shoot you, and set you up to take the fall on the whole thing."

"I couldn't be arrested for killing Deirdre. I have a watertight alibi."

"And a whole lot of cash withdrawals over the last few months to cover your gambling debts. How hard do you think it would be to make it look like you paid someone to kill her?"

Hallings slumped in the doorway and his face went pale.

"I don't believe you."

"Who do you think tipped off the police that Deirdre was dead to begin with? Someone who wanted to set you up."

That part of my tale was a lie—it had been the tweakers stealing copper who found her—but I wanted to throw a little more doubt into Hallings's thought process.

Hallings looked troubled, but he wasn't ready to believe any story that included Kendra's participation.

"You can't prove anything," he said.

"Actually, yes. I can."

"And we can offer you a better out," Chava said. "Let me call Careno."

Hallings rubbed his face. He looked exhausted and slightly ill. Clearly none of this made sense to him. He did, however, manage to keep his gun pointed roughly in our direction.

"Okay. On speaker. No funny business. No trying to call the police or whatever."

Chava nodded. "But I need a phone." I waited, not wanting him to know I had mine on me.

"Stand against that wall." Hallings gestured at me. "Back against the wall. You shoot me, I shoot you too." He pointed his gun at me. "I might be able to shoot you both before you can take me out. Keep in mind I've got nothing to lose."

I did what he asked while he pulled out his cell and placed it on the desk. Then he took a step back. "Okay," he said. "Do it."

"I need to free her so she can use the phone," I said.

"No," Hallings said. "You can press the buttons for her."

I looked at Chava, who shrugged and recited a number from memory.

"Speaker phone," Hallings reminded us. I pressed the buttons and soon we could all hear the sound of the phone ringing.

The phone picked up, but no voice came on the line.

"Rudy?" Chava spoke into the phone.

Rudy? The name of whomever Chava called to get her information on the Mob?

"Yeah?" a voice said.

"Chava here. Sorry, I know it's a little early. I need a favor."

"Okay."

"I need to set up a meet with Vincent Careno."

For a moment nothing came over the phone but the sound of Rudy breathing. I had no idea what Chava was doing, but I sure hoped this Rudy would play along.

"When?"

"Soon. If he's still here in Bellingham, today would be great. The sooner the better."

"Okay. Should I call you back on this number?"

"ASAP," Chava said.

"Sit tight."

We could hear the phone go dead on Rudy's end so I clicked the end call button on Hallings's phone as well.

"See?" Chava said. "Nothing to it."

"We'll just have to wait and see what happens if he calls back," Hallings said.

"*When* he calls back."

"How long will this take?" Hallings asked. "Leeds is supposed to be back soon."

"Leeds is not coming back soon," I said, ever helpful. "And you might as well start calling him Turner; that's his real name." I wanted him to distrust Turner even more than he distrusted me.

"You don't know that. He said he'd be here soon."

"He's in my car too."

"Now I know you're bullshitting me," Hallings said, stepping closer again, gun hand outstretched.

"Okay, okay, just calm down," I said. "We'll do it your way. We'll just wait for Rudy to call back." I couldn't make him look in my car and I hoped somehow Rudy would get the situation diffused. For now, I just needed to get the gun away from Hallings.

"That's right," Hallings said. "We're all just going to sit tight. And you," he shook his gun at me, "are going to stop talking to me!"

"I'm feeling a little faint," Chava said, and I looked at her, concerned. Her color looked good, but I didn't want to take any chances.

"I'm just going to ease her down," I said to Hallings, who nodded it was okay.

"Whatever. Just stop talking to me."

While I helped Chava slide down the wall, she looked intently at the space below the desk again. I followed her line of sight and saw a paperclip on the floor.

I had a pretty good idea what Chava could do with a paperclip and a pair of handcuffs.

I got her situated and took my time pulling her feet out in front of her.

"Better?" I asked.

"I think I should lie down on my side," she said. "I'm still feeling a little faint."

"Here, let me help you," I said. Pulling her down on to the floor, I got her halfway behind the desk, with the weight off her hands. Hallings stood in the doorway, half his attention on the doors to the outside and half on us. Clearly the man wasn't used to this kind of situation. He was dying to see if Kendra really was outside, but couldn't figure out how to check. He and I were at a standoff, both armed and refusing to budge, but not wanting the other to shoot.

I grabbed the paperclip and slid it into Chava's hands. I didn't have time to straighten it out because Hallings might see what I was doing. Then I pulled Turner's gun out from my waistband—where I'd tucked it earlier when I'd taken mine out—and stuck that under the desk where Chava could see it.

She took the paperclip and winked at me.

Fifteen long minutes later, the cell rang again. Hallings nodded at me and I put the phone back on speaker, holding it out to Chava where she lay on the floor.

"He said he can meet you tonight at the casino. Does that work for you?"

"Yes," Chava said.

Did my mother really have access to the Mob? I guess I shouldn't be surprised, given the Cha-Cha bit. Just who was this Rudy person, anyway?

"Nine o'clock. Just sit tight where you are until then." Chava's mystery man hung up the phone.

"We can't just sit here," Hallings said. "Not with Leeds coming back."

"Turner is not coming back," I said again. "He's in my car. Why don't we all just go on out there together and I'll show you."

"I don't trust you."

"Look. Leave my mother in here; she's bound up. You and I will go outside and I'll show you Kendra and Turner."

My priority was to get Chava safe; after that, the rest of this mess could sort itself out.

Before I could do anything else, another voice said from behind Hallings, "Karl isn't your biggest problem."

"Kendra! You're safe. How did you get away from Careno?" Hallings said, turning away from us just as I heard a click that told me Chava had one side of the handcuffs unlocked.

"Why, Matt? Why did you sleep with Deirdre?"

Were we really back to that?

"What are you talking about?"

"If you had just stayed faithful, none of this would have happened."

Hallings's shoulders slumped. "She was telling the truth, wasn't she?" he said with a shrug toward me. "You and Deirdre were working together with this Turner guy to set me up. How could you?"

"I wasn't working with them to begin with, not until you started up with her."

"She didn't mean anything to me," Hallings said, lowering his gun. "It was a mistake. I never would have left you for her."

I slowly moved away from the desk and raised my own

weapon. I wanted a clear shot on Hallings if I thought he was going to lose it, but without shooting Kendra.

"Cheating was one thing, but now you're just lying about it," she said.

And then she shot him too.

Chapter Thirty-Two

—•—

I SHOULD HAVE KNOWN SHE was the one more likely to actually shoot someone. This time, however, Kendra missed, and now Hallings was really mad.

"You tried to shoot me!" he said, barreling down on Kendra. She might have gotten another shot off, but didn't react quickly enough, and he tackled her to the floor in the roasting room. The two struggled and I followed, yelling at them to stop before one of them did something stupid and irreparable.

"Freeze! Both of you."

The two of them continued fighting on the floor, both of their guns going off, shots pinging off the sides of metal vats. They continued struggling, however, so I didn't think either was hurt too badly, though I heard Hallings grunt as if he might have been winged. Hallings dropped his own gun and grabbed onto Kendra's, while Kendra slapped, pinched, and clawed at him like a wild animal with her free hand. Despite her diminutive size, my money might have been on Kendra, even if she was in a family way.

Just then, the back door flung open and Karl Turner threw himself into the room, breaking up Hallings and Kendra. The three of them rolled away from one another. Karl picked up Hallings's gun and pointed it back and forth between Kendra and Hallings. Hallings, in his struggle to get free of the line of fire, ploughed into me, sending me onto my butt in a bone-jarring thump. Managing to hold on to my own weapon, I pushed the big man off me and threw myself sideways, out of the line of fire. I looked around for Chava, and saw she'd gotten herself safely tucked up behind the heavy wooden desk.

Crawling to the edge of the doorway I peered out into the other room.

Karl stood over Kendra, Hallings's gun trained on her with a surprisingly steady hand given the gunshot wound he'd received earlier.

"You should have come with me, Kendra," he said. "You had a chance to fix this. When we were in the car. You and I could have been on the way to Canada right now. But no, you had to come in here. For what, a little revenge? Didn't I teach you anything? Revenge is pointless."

"Really?" Kendra asked him, aiming her own gun at him for yet another standoff. "Then why are you here? Why didn't you run when I gave you the chance?"

Karl looked up and saw me in the doorway. He brought Hallings's gun up to point at me again. I guess he thought I was more of a danger than Kendra; after all, she hadn't done much damage so far.

So I shot Karl.

Karl looked surprised and dropped like a stone. I rushed over and took Hallings's gun out of his hand.

"Enough is enough," I said, surveying the damage, a nice clean through and through of his right arm above the elbow. Not a bad shot considering he was moving at the time.

"You'll live," I said, turning to check on Hallings and Kendra, only to find Kendra standing with her gun trained on me.

"You've gotta be kidding me, Kendra. Put the gun down."

"No, Eddie. I've done my good deed for the day, I helped you find your mother, but you are going to let me walk out of here, right now."

"Why on earth did you let Turner out of my car?"

"I didn't want you turning him over to the police. I didn't want him talking. I thought he'd run."

Strike two for Kendra.

"It's all over, Kendra," I said. "Put the gun down. Haven't we had enough shooting for one night?"

"I'm shot, Kendra," Hallings said. "You don't want me to die. I need help."

"You," Kendra said looking down at her husband. "You were supposed to be my white knight. You were supposed to save me, and look at the mess you've made."

I really wanted to tell Kendra she was part of the mess-making, but now didn't seem to be the time. Kendra was raising her gun again and pointing it toward Hallings.

"I should shoot you again for cheating on me."

"Kendra, you are not going to shoot anyone," I said from my place in the doorway. Unfortunately this had the effect of her turning her gun on me.

The sound of the gunshot startled us all, but no one more than Kendra; she looked stunned as the spot of blood appeared through her shirt. I swiveled around and saw my mother standing behind me, Turner's gun in her hands.

"You?" Kendra said before she crumpled to the ground next to Hallings.

"Baby!" Hallings said, pulling Kendra to him. "Are you all right?"

"That hurt!" Kendra said as I went to her.

"Let me see," I said, tearing her shirt open.

"The bullet just nicked you, Kendra. You're going to be fine. Here," I said, tearing a strip of cloth from Kendra's now tattered shirt. "Hold pressure on her." I handed the cloth to Hallings. "Unless you're hurt too badly." I had almost forgotten Kendra's wild shot had struck him first.

"I'll be okay," Hallings said, ministering to his wife. "You really cared enough that I slept with Deirdre to want to shoot me?" He looked deep into his wife's eyes. "I didn't know you loved me that much."

"I do, baby," Kendra crooned, wincing as he pushed on her wound. "It tore me up inside."

Oh, brother. This couldn't be happening.

"Are you done shooting people?" I asked her. She nodded and I took the gun from her hand.

"Eddie?" I heard my mother's voice from where she'd slumped down in the doorway.

"Coming, Chava," I said. "That was a hell of a shot. But it's over. Everything is going to be all right."

"I'm not so sure of that," Chava said. "I think I've been shot too."

Chapter Thirty-Three

———•———

SCRAMBLING OVER TO THE DOORWAY, I began to check over my mother. I could see a puddle of blood underneath her, but I couldn't find the entrance wound.

"It's going to be all right," I said. "Let me call 911 and get an ambulance here."

Even as I spoke, I could hear sirens in the distance.

"Someone must have heard the gunshots," I said. "That was awful fast."

"Rudy came through," Chava said, right before she slipped into unconsciousness.

I located the hole on her side, and put pressure on it while I waited for the cavalry to arrive.

THE POLICE AND AN AMBULANCE arrived a moment later. The building must have looked like a scene from a Bruce Willis movie with all the bodies scattered around. The only thing that mattered to me was getting help for my mother.

The police came through and secured the scene, with the EMTs following after. I surrendered all the guns—Kendra's, Hallings's, and mine, which I had, and Turner's, which Chava had used—and demanded immediate attention for Chava. One of the EMTs attended to my mother with my help, while a second one checked on the other three. After we got Chava stabilized, a police officer put me in the back of his patrol car until a detective could arrive on the scene and sort out what happened. The sun had come up while we'd been inside, and the day had dawned cold and clear.

I knew it would be Chance Parker even before he drove up. It had been that kind of night. He got out of the car with his partner. The two of them talked for a few minutes before Kate went into the building and Chance walked over to me.

"Nice to see you again, Eddie," he said, sliding into the front seat of the patrol car and looking at me through the wire mesh between the seats.

"You too, Chance," I said. "What's the matter," I patted the protective screen between us, "Afraid of little old me?"

"Very much so," he said closing the door and starting up the engine to give us a little heat. "You must be freezing in ... that." He gave my shorts and shower shoes an amused look. I figured he could smell the fumes from the oil stains on my t-shirt.

"It was self-defense," I said.

"How many people did you shoot in there?" he asked.

"Just one. He pointed his gun at me."

"I think you need to get me up to speed."

"Where do you want me to start?" I asked.

"How about the beginning?"

"First, I want to know how my mother is," I said. "Then I'll tell you everything."

"Your mom is going to be fine."

"What about Karl Turner?"

"Is he the guy with two gunshot wounds?"

"He is," I said.

"One of those bullet holes yours?"

"Yes." I thought about events for a long moment. How much trouble was I in? I hadn't exactly been an angel with Turner.

"Is Turner dead?" I asked. Chance just looked at me, with no expression.

He finally broke the silence. "Are you sure you aren't hurt, Eddie?" I heard actual concern in his voice. Maybe there was hope for us yet.

I nodded.

"Turner will live."

"How did the police know to come here?" I asked.

"You'll have to ask your mother," he said. "For now, I want to hear your side of the story. We're going downtown and I'm going to take your statement."

"Someone needs to get my dog out of my car," I said. "He probably needs water and a pee. Or at least bring my car down to the station."

"You have a dog?"

"I think so. He doesn't have a collar or tags or anything. You can't take him to the pound. I'll never get him out again."

Chance looked pained.

"Please, Chance. It's not for me. It's for him."

Was it a him? I hadn't checked out his parts. I'd assumed he was masculine because of his size, but maybe it was a her.

I was going to have to learn more about dogs.

"Fine. I'll take care of it."

I hoped Chance would keep his promise after he saw how big, dirty, and hairy the dog was.

I GAVE CHANCE THE WHOLE story. I kept it short and succinct, nothing more than the bare basics. Though I did explain why I didn't call the police.

"Kendra hadn't been exactly forthcoming," I said to Chance. "For all I knew I'd find out she had made up the whole 'I'm being held against my will,' as a way to placate her angry husband."

Chance closed his eyes and shook his head. "Go on," was all he said.

When I got to the shooting at my house, Chance put his hand up to stop me.

"There's a third crime scene?"

I nodded. Much as I didn't want my house taken over by the Crime Scene Investigation Unit—fingerprint dust is a bear to clean up—I figured I'd better be as honest I as could. With so many players involved, anything I tried to leave out would no doubt emerge later and make me look guilty of some crime.

That wouldn't help me patch things up with Chance.

By the time I finished the entire story, I was exhausted, and Chance didn't look much better. I'd gotten an update from Chance's partner Kate partway through the interview, that Chava was going to fine, but I was still anxious to see her for myself.

"Let me make sure I've got this straight," Chance said when I ended with his arrival on the scene at the coffee roaster. "Kendra went with Karl voluntarily, but later changed her mind and was held against her will." I nodded, so he continued, "She called you with information about where she was held, so you went there to help her."

Okay, so I hadn't been totally honest. Chance hadn't asked the right questions to elicit the information from me that I'd broken into the house Karl was staying in to track down her whereabouts.

Chance took my silence for agreement.

"While you were freeing Kendra, Karl grabbed your mother. He told you to meet at your house. Fearing for your mother's life, you agreed not to contact the police. Once you were all at your house, Kendra shot Karl, but only when she thought her own life was in danger. Then she figured out where your mother was held." I nodded again and Chance continued to outline the events as they happened.

"Lastly, your mother shot Kendra."

"In self-defense," I said. "Kendra's gun was pointed in Chava's direction." I left out that Chava might have actually been protecting me, not herself. The trajectories of the gunshot would support my story. Chava had been directly behind me, so we were both in the line of fire. The law gets a little stickier when someone shoots in defense of another person.

"Okay," he said when he finished. "Write it all out and sign it."

He tossed a legal pad down and left the room. When I was done, he came back in and told me I was free to go. "I advise you to stay away from anything else to do with this case," he said. "We aren't charging you with anything, but that could change if we find out you lied about any of part of your story."

I nodded.

"Since your house is also currently a crime scene, you'll have to stay elsewhere," he added. I could imagine my little house being torn apart by the police. They'd want to make sure there wasn't any evidence I'd known Turner or the Hallings outside of my investigation of Matthew. Proof there was more to the story than I was letting on. At least there wasn't anything to find, right?

Unless Kendra had given me something I didn't know about and the police would find it somewhere in my house. Was that even possible?

"Where's the dog?" I asked, realizing there was nothing I could do except wait out the investigation.

"I thought Kate was going to have a fit when she saw him, but you're lucky she's a dog lover. We've got him situated in an interrogation room," Chance said, shaking his head. "Please take him with you."

Walking into the small room where the dog was, I wondered what kind of reception I'd get. The mountain made a funny sound and rolled over on his back, tail wagging, tongue hanging out of his mouth.

Definitely a boy.

I went over and knelt down at his side, rubbing the coarse fur on his tummy.

"Who's a good boy?" I said, surprising myself with the baby talk. Where did that voice come from?

"Your car is in impound," Chance told me. "You'll get it back when we're done collecting evidence. I find it interesting that Karl chose to ride in the way back of the car instead of the backseat." I knew he was considering a kidnapping charge on Karl Turner, but I was in the clear where that was concerned.

"Would you get into the backseat with him?" I gestured toward the dog, who smelled like a cross between road kill and a wet sheep. "Can I get a ride to the car rental agency? There's no way a cab will let me bring *el perro* here." I wasn't sure why I used the Spanish word for "dog." Maybe my father's reappearance had set something off in my linguistic considerations.

I'd have to figure out a name for him at some point. I'd never named anything in my life, not even imaginary friends when I was a kid.

Chance gave me a long look, then sighed. Heavily. "You really are a pain in the ass, Eddie."

"But you've missed me, haven't you?" I didn't look up from my spot on the floor next to the dog, not wanting to see the look on his face. I didn't think he'd respond, so his quiet words took me by surprise.

"Just a little bit."

I GOT A RENTAL CAR and checked on Chava at the hospital. She was knocked out on pain meds, so I left her a note saying I'd be back the next day, and *el perro* and I headed out for a hotel that allowed dogs. Using a rope for a leash, I snuck him into the room so they wouldn't see how big he was, as their rules said "dogs up to eighty pounds allowed." I also didn't want them to know I planned to give his doggy-dreads a good shampoo in their tub.

It went better than I thought it would, though I did have to pull a lot of hair out of the drain before I took a shower myself.

Then I slept for twelve hours. I only got up when *el perro* poked me with his nose to say he needed to go out. We went to the pet store for basic supplies, and I got a call from Chance I could have my house back. His voice felt good in my ear.

"How bad's the mess?" I asked.

"I asked the technicians to be gentle," he said.

There was a moment of dead air between us and I tried to think of a way to extend the conversation.

"So you solved your first homicide case in Bellingham," I finally came up with. "Congratulations."

"Thanks," he said. "Not how I thought we'd reconnect."

So he'd thought about us reconnecting?

"I'd love to buy you a drink," I said, my optimism buoyed by his comment. "You know, to celebrate."

Another long pause. Had I pushed too soon?

"I'll let you know," he said before ending the call.

I looked over at *el perro*. "What does that mean?" I asked him. The dog tilted his head as if considering my question. He gave a short bark as if to say he didn't have an answer. "I don't know either, buddy. Let's go home."

Given how long I'd slept, it was late in the day when I finally arrived home. The winter sun long vanished from the sky.

Walking up to my front door, I could see I definitely had some cleaning up to do. Crime scene tape crossed the door, though it had been pulled away now the house had been released. I stepped inside, feeling the heat had been turned back up. Thinking Chava must have jacked up the temperature before we'd left, or the crime scene investigators wanted it warmer, I started over to the thermostat to turn the heat down.

"How do you live with it so cold in here?" a voice said. I'd only heard it once, but I recognized it immediately. *El perro* sat down without a sound, making me wonder just what kind of guard dog he'd make.

"Hi ..." I paused. The flippant "Dad" I'd said at the casino didn't feel appropriate, but I couldn't call him Mr. Zapata.

He laughed, obviously amused at my indecision.

"Eduardo will do fine," he said. "Come, sit. You've had a rough couple of days."

"I have," I said, sliding onto the sofa next to him.

"Who is this?" he asked, gesturing at my furry companion.

"It's a long story, but he saved my life."

"Well," Eduardo said, reaching out to scratch the ears of the dog, who'd settled at my feet, apparently unconcerned about being faced with a member of the Mafia. "That's a good dog then, isn't it?"

I hadn't had time to think about the fact I'd ruined the plans the Mafia had for Matthew Hallings's car dealership. I wondered if my father, the butcher—or the cleaner or the candlestick maker or whatever he was—had arrived here to take a pound of flesh for my indiscretion.

"Eddie Shoes," my father said. I didn't know him well enough to read the tone in his voice. "*Zapata* means cobbler, you know," he said continuing to scratch the dog's ears. "Not shoes, that would be *zapatos*," he finished with a heavy accent on the O.

"Eddie Cobbler? I'd sound like a pie." This popped out of my mouth without any thought process on my part. Had I really just said that to the man?

Eduardo looked up at me, and I thought I saw surprise in his face, then more laughter, which felt genuine. "This is true. Maybe Cobbler is not so good a choice. Shoes, that's close enough, is it not?"

He continued looking at me, his hand still on the ruff of the dog's neck. Was he really curious about me? After all this time? He didn't forget me when he left Chava behind? I debated about how much to tell him. Did he really want to know?

"When I moved away from Spokane," I said, deciding to tell him something Chava didn't know, "I wanted to be someone new."

"New, but still connected to your past."

I had never thought about it that way before, but I had to admit he was right.

"What can I do for you, Eduardo?" I asked after he sat quietly for a while, clearly in no hurry to explain his sudden, and slightly disconcerting, appearance in my house. Did he just come by to catch up on the last thirty years? Ask me why Shoes and not Cobbler? Something told me there was a little more to his visit than that.

"I thought you might be curious, what my associates were going to do, about the arrangements we've made for the debt owed by Hallings."

"The arrangements I've thrown a wrench into."

"You have at that, haven't you, *mija*," he said with a chuckle. Who knew my father would have a sense of humor?

"Am I on the hook for it?"

Eduardo leaned back in the sofa, leaving the dog to doze off at our feet. "What good would that do us? You aren't in any position to either pay us back or help us out. No. We have other ways to make good on it."

"Who gets the dealership?" I asked, wondering if that was already known information despite the events happening so recently.

"The Hallings, I assume," he said, "though I anticipate it may require some silent partners for him to hang on to it throughout his legal troubles."

"The Hallings? You mean they're staying together?"

"I believe so," Eduardo said. "There may be some mutual benefits for them to do so. Spousal privilege and all that."

"How much jail time do you think they'll see?" I asked.

"Not as much as you might think," my father said. "It appears most of the crimes in this … situation … were committed by this Karl Turner. Kendra and Hallings were victims. Hallings had the foresight to tape all his conversations with Turner on a machine in his office. Those tapes make Turner look very, very guilty."

That explained the clicking sounds in Hallings's home office.

What happened to the recordings of his conversations with Careno? Had those conveniently disappeared before the police showed up at his house with a search warrant?

"Karl may have another story," I said. "Once he wakes up."

"He won't be telling anyone any stories," Eduardo said. "Karl Turner did not survive his surgery."

That stopped me short. Had I killed the man? He didn't seem badly hurt when he'd left the coffee roaster, and I'd heard he came through surgery okay. Why hadn't Chance called to tell me that?

"He had a very bad allergic reaction to a medication he was given. Unfortunately, he did not survive."

"That's awfully lucky for the Hallings."

"I suppose so."

"Were you at the hospital when this happened?" I asked before I really thought through what I was asking. I had to be tired to open that can of worms.

That darn curiosity of mine ... I wondered for a moment which side of the family tree I got that aspect of my personality.

"It's amazing how invisible a Latino can be in this culture, don't you think? You look like me. Perhaps you have experienced that?"

A memory flashed through my mind. I was just a kid, but it involved someone calling me *spic*, long before I knew what the word meant. I remembered Chava stepping in front of me. "That's my daughter you're denigrating," she'd said. I had to look *denigrating* up in the dictionary. I'd looked up *spic* too, but couldn't find it at the time.

"I haven't," I said.

Eduardo shrugged like he didn't believe me, but wasn't going to challenge my response. "A man like me, I can become a janitor, or a day worker, or say, an orderly at a hospital, and no one looks twice."

A shiver ran down my spine. It didn't feel quite safe he was giving me this information, even if we did look so much alike.

"I tell you this for a reason," he continued, as if he were reading my mind.

"What's that?"

"We are done here, my colleagues and myself. We are going home, for the time being. I think we'll all be better off if no more investigations are done on behalf of this Kendra Hallings. She is out of danger. The bad man is dead. And you and your mother are safe and sound as well. We should all just leave it at that, don't you think? Let the police do their jobs."

"I've already gotten my one free pass ... is that what you're saying?"

"Something like that."

"I appreciate the warning."

"Don't think of it as a warning. Think of it as fatherly advice."

With that, he rose and crossed over to the thermostat, which he turned back down to where I kept it set.

"Can I ask you one thing?" I said before he left. After all, I might never see the man again.

"You can ask," he said, "though that doesn't mean I will answer."

"Chava thought you didn't know she was pregnant, but you've known about me all along. Why did you leave?"

I think my question surprised him, though I don't know what he expected.

"Your grandfather knew. He came to me and told me to leave. He knew I wasn't the right man to be a father to a child."

"How would he know that?"

"Your grandfather had exceptional insight into human nature. How could he not with what he endured?"

"So you left? Because my Opa told you to?"

"Not because he told me to, but because he was right. You and Chava were better off without me. No?"

"And you were better off without us?"

My father went still and looked at me for a long moment.

His mouth was hard, but the look in his eyes was soft.

"You might have been good in the family business, *mija*," he said, "but that might not have been good for you."

With that he left.

My breathing returned to normal, and something finally registered in my mind.

He'd never removed his gloves. I couldn't prove he'd been here. He'd come and gone like a ghost.

Was he a ghost I would see again one day?

Chapter Thirty-Four

———◆———

"RUDY HAD THE CELLPHONE TRACED," Chava explained the next morning, as I sat next to her bedside.

"How did Rudy know you needed him to do that?"

"He knew from my calling that particular number I was in trouble. He had the phone we called from located with GPS and contacted the authorities here."

"Is he in the Mob?" I asked, feeling slightly lightheaded.

Chava laughed. "No, dear. I don't have that much of a connection to Vincent Careno. I just made all that up. Rudy is a Fed."

"In Vegas?" I asked.

"Of course, darling. That is where I lived."

I didn't even flinch at the past tense.

"How is it you're so close to this Fed that you can call him up and he can read your mind?"

"I do have friends, Eddie," Chava said with a smile. "He's a lovely man. I'll have to introduce you to him one of these days."

"He's not a practicing Jew by any chance," I asked, wondering if he was the cause of her sudden interest in our heritage.

"He might be," she said.

I told Chava I had to go down the hall to check on Kendra. I'd heard she wanted to talk to me. I left Chava happily shuffling cards to pass the time.

Kendra's gunshot wound hadn't been serious, but it did require minor surgery, so she lay in a hospital bed just down the hall from my mother. Now she was just waiting to be released from the hospital. Walking up to her room, I nodded at the guard stationed out front—a young, blonde woman who didn't look old enough to have graduated from the police academy.

"She awake?

"Who are you?"

"She's my client." I thought maybe the police officer, as inexperienced as she was, might assume I was an attorney.

"I'm not sure I'm allowed to let you in.

"This will just take a minute."

"She's being detained."

"So I can go in to see her at your discretion."

The young woman started to say something else—perhaps she was going to ask why I hadn't come out and said I was Kendra's attorney—when the door to Kendra's room opened and Chance Parker came out.

"Thank you, Linda," Chance said to the young woman before he noticed me standing nearby.

He nodded at me, his face unreadable. I guess now wasn't the time he was going to take me up on having that drink.

"Your mother is doing well?" he said.

"She is."

"Good."

"Thank you."

We stood there awkwardly, the young beat cop watching our short volley of words go back and forth like she was a spectator at Wimbledon.

Before Chance could ask what I was doing in front of Kendra's room after he specifically told me to stay out of the case, Iz walked around the corner from the elevators. Her eyes shifted back and forth between Chance and me and I could see her take in the tension. She carried a bouquet of flowers.

"Hey, Eddie. I just came to give your mother my well wishes," she said. She handed the bouquet of flowers to Chance, which gave her the freedom to sweep me into a hug. "I'm so glad you're all right."

"Thank you. That's so thoughtful," I said gesturing at the flowers.

"Hi, Detective Parker," she said, taking the bouquet back from him. "Are you here to check on Chava too?"

Chance looked unsure of how to answer. Iz's actions had interrupted what would no doubt have been his upbraiding of me for my attempt to get in to see Kendra.

"I, uh, that is ..." Chance stumbled for the right words. Izabelle had that effect on people.

"I'm sure you're as glad as I am Eddie's momma will have a full recovery."

"Of course," Chance said, regaining his composure. "I'll stop in to see her before I leave the hospital."

"Room 312," I said.

"We can go together," she said taking Chance's arm and leading him the other direction. "She may need her rest and this way we only interrupt her once."

In that moment I realized how much I appreciated my friend.

"Why are you trying to see Kendra, Eddie?" Chance asked, when I made no move to join them.

"I need to talk to her." I said, hoping Chance would give the okay. Maybe he'd argue with me less with Iz listening in.

"Why?"

"She could have run," I said. "She didn't. That's part of what saved my mother's life."

"Except, your mother wouldn't have been in danger in the first place if Kendra hadn't gotten mixed up in all of this, right?"

Why did he have to be so practical?

"True."

I waited. I didn't want to beg, but I also needed to get in and find out what Karl thought I had. It was the last piece of the puzzle and damned if I was going to let it go.

Chance looked back and forth between Iz and me. I knew he didn't want to start an argument in front of Iz in the middle of the hospital, and maybe he thought he'd learn something from my conversation with Kendra.

"Give her fifteen minutes," Chance said to the young policewoman, handing her a voice recorder. "Record the entire conversation. When her time is up, kick her out."

His words were softened by the wink he gave me, which happened so fast I almost missed it.

He let Iz lead him away from the room. I tried not to think about all the embarrassing things my mother might say to Chance, and just considered myself lucky Iz had showed up and diffused the tension. He might not have been so amenable to letting me talk to his suspect otherwise.

Kendra lay small and frail in the hospital bed. Covered in white sheets and a white blanket, she looked almost angelic, the big doe eyes standing out even more in a face that was pale and drawn. Linda stood on the other side of the bed, voice recorder out. She turned it on as I walked up to Kendra's side.

"How are you feeling?" I asked.

Kendra rattled the handcuff attached to her wrist and the rail of the bed.

"Trapped."

"Well, you did shoot a few people."

Kendra smiled at that, but a tear rolled down the side of her face. I wondered if this one was real or not. She might still be playing on my sympathy, even though I couldn't help her now.

"You're going to recover at least," I said, knowing that wasn't really the issue here.

"So I can go to jail."

"What about the baby? Was it hurt?"

"I can't talk about that right now," she said, turning her head away, glancing at the policewoman standing over her.

I wondered if she'd lost it and was grieving, or if she faced having it in jail.

"So what was Karl talking about?" I asked, deciding I needed to change the subject. There wasn't much to be done about her upcoming trial or plea deal and subsequent prison sentence, unless my father was right, and she'd be considered a victim in all of this. I was careful to voice my question as vaguely as possible for the tape Chance would listen to later.

"I don't know," Kendra said, turning her wide eyes back to me. "He kept talking crazy about that, but I have no idea what he was after. But that's not what I wanted to talk about."

I wasn't sure how to get her to stop lying to me. Maybe I'd never know what he thought I had.

"So tell me the truth, you were in on it all along, weren't you?" I didn't pursue what she wanted to talk about, but sat down, holding Kendra's attention. I hoped she'd forget Linda stood nearby recording her every word. She moved her arm again, trying to rearrange herself around the handcuff. It clinked when she moved.

"Not about kidnapping your mother, or killing Deirdre. Karl did those things on his own. That's when I got scared—when I realized what he was capable of."

I must not have looked convinced.

"It wasn't right, killing someone who was working with him."

"You mean someone like you?" Kendra looked away again. I guess I'd hit a nerve. "Wait," I said, thinking about how she phrased her sentence. "He'd killed before?"

"Not someone he knew!" A look I couldn't read crossed her face. "Well, not someone he liked."

"I don't think you understand the meaning of *psychopath*, Kendra. They don't *like* anyone. They are incapable of that emotion. People are either useful or not useful."

"Maybe," Kendra said, unconvinced.

"He couldn't imagine you leaving him, that's all. It wasn't love."

Kendra's chin trembled and I expected to see tears fall, but apparently when they were real she held them back. She closed her eyes and they remained, her lashes sparkling.

"You wanted to tell me something?" I said after it became clear she wasn't going to speak again.

She looked at me and turned on the little girl charm one last time. "I helped you get your mother back. That has to count for something."

"Oh, I get it. You want my help. What is it you think I can do? I don't have any sway with the judge."

"You could talk to the prosecutor. You could tell her how I helped. I just went along with Karl a little because I was afraid of him." She spoke these last words into the recorder Linda held. I guess she thought that would help her in some way.

"That's a tough sell given how long you and Karl were in cahoots. Besides, you can tell her yourself." I got up to walk out of the room, tired of Kendra's "poor me" persona.

"I wasn't even sixteen when I started working for him," Kendra said, her voice both stronger and more vulnerable at the same time. "Fifteen, Eddie. How much choice did I really have? I left home because there was no one looking out for me there. Do you know my dad didn't even try to find me after I took off?"

Turning around, I could see Kendra half rising out of the bed in her agitation. She was so intent on getting through to me that she didn't notice the red marks appearing on her pale wrist where she leaned against the handcuffs and had forgotten the police officer in the room.

"You're going to hurt yourself," I said, sitting down next to her again. She lay back on the bed and I rearranged the IVs that had gotten tangled in the sheets.

"Karl saw me coming a mile away. He realized what I could do for him. The men I could manipulate with my body, the women I could manipulate with my scared little girl act."

"Yeah, I've seen that one first hand," I said, but my anger had abated.

"By the time I turned eighteen, I didn't know any other life. What was I going to do? Flip burgers? I never finished high school, I had no skills beyond …."

I watched her drift off into memories I wasn't sure I wanted to share.

"Besides," she said with a small laugh, a real one I hadn't heard before. "I'd gotten used to the life. The art of the scam. Karl had that right. He was proud of me, Eddie. I know you might not understand, but no one ever was before."

In that moment I realized how lucky I was. Chava might not have been perfect, but she always knew where I was. If I'd run away, she would have had the bloodhounds on my trail immediately, ready to drag me back with her own hands. Once I was an adult I could make my own decisions, but not at fifteen. I might not have had a normal childhood, but I was never lost. Not like Kendra, who remained lost even now.

And what if I'd run into a Karl Turner instead of a Benjamin Cooper? I might have turned to a life of crime myself. I could always justify my actions for the greater good, but I knew I walked a fine line.

There but for the grace of Chava and Coop ….

"Okay. You win. I'll talk to the prosecutor. I'll let them know my mother might have died without your help."

"*Would* have died without my help," Kendra said with a smile.

"Don't push your luck."

AFTER LEAVING KENDRA'S ROOM, I walked over to the nurses' station. I knew they couldn't discuss Kendra's medical condition with me, but I thought I'd give it a try anyway. Maybe they would let something slip.

"I wanted to ask about the baby," I said to a nurse standing at the station reading a chart.

"Baby? What baby?" she asked.

"Kendra Hallings." I gestured at the guard sitting outside

Kendra's room. "The gunshot wound. I know it wasn't serious, but I wondered if it damaged her pregnancy?"

"Pregnancy?" The woman looked very confused.

"She's pregnant. That must have come up during her surgery."

The nurse looked at another woman sitting behind the desk, who shrugged back at her, equally confused.

"Are you family?"

"No."

"We can't discuss a patient's condition with you."

"Right. Sorry."

I walked around the corner and stopped at a drinking fountain, wondering about the nurse's reaction. I could hear the two of them talking and paused for a little eavesdropping.

"Pregnant? Where did she get that idea?" the first woman said. I couldn't hear the response from the woman behind the desk. I leaned a little closer to the edge of the wall.

"That woman hasn't had the plumbing for a baby in a long time. I don't know when she had that hysterectomy, but I do know those things don't grow back."

I could hear the two of them laughing as I walked away.

Strike three. Kendra was out.

IN MY OFFICE THE NEXT morning, I moved Kendra's file into my archives. Chava was getting discharged and I was supposed to be at the hospital at 11:00 to pick her up. *El perro* had been given a clean bill of health from a veterinarian and a visit to a groomer had worked wonders. He was still a shaggy beast, but he looked much better with a bit of a trim.

"Irish Wolfhound and Tibetan Mastiff is my guess," the vet had said when I'd inquired about the breed. He weighed in at one-hundred-fifty pounds and the vet assured me he would put on a few more with a regular diet. His condition made the vet assume the dog had been alone for quite some time.

I still hadn't made a decision about what to do with him, but my "Dog Found" ads hadn't come up with anyone ready to claim him, nor had my calls to the local shelters. He'd taken up residence on the sofa in my office, apparently feeling right at home. Watching him sleep, I let my mind go back to the question of Turner wanting something Kendra had given me. He was so adamant about it.

And Kendra had wanted very badly to get back into my office.

I looked around, but Kendra hadn't been there without me present. She couldn't have hidden anything without my seeing her do it.

Except in the bathroom. Where she'd spent a lot of time that last visit fixing her makeup after bursting into tears.

I found it taped up with Band-Aids underneath the toilet lid. A small red plastic flash drive. Plugging it into my computer, I started going through the files it contained. Bank accounts, passwords, the money trail. All the information needed to access Karl Turner's rather sizeable fortune. And photos of Kendra and Karl.

Proof she'd been his partner from the beginning. Maybe Kendra wasn't going to get so lucky after all. I now had all the evidence I needed to show she'd been in it from the start. Even Matthew Hallings would have trouble disputing this.

"YOU DID THE RIGHT THING," Chava said when I told her about handing the flash drive over to Chance Parker. We were in her room waiting for the doctor to give the final okay on her discharge.

"We could have retired with that kind of money," I said, only half joking. "And I never did get paid a cent on this stupid case."

I'd told Chava about the cash in the cosmetics pouch and how the police found nothing when they went through my car. Kendra apparently took it before she came in my house and shot Karl, hiding it somewhere nearby to retrieve later. I'd been careless to let her see I had it when I'd gotten stuff out of my glove box, but I'd had other things on my mind. She also cleared out the real estate files I'd removed from the house Turner had been staying in. I wasn't going to mention either of those items to the police. I'd have to explain how I'd come by them.

"Much better Kendra does time. I can't believe she lied about being pregnant. Setting you up."

"Almost getting you killed."

"That too. Do you think Turner would have killed Kendra? Once he got his flash drive back?"

"Maybe. But Kendra sure seems to have an ability to bend men around her little finger."

Not to mention me.

"Will Hallings finally see through her little act? Their marriage did survive her trying to shoot him."

"Yeah, this time I think she's done. The photos of her and Turner are very … indiscreet."

"Well, there's that then," Chava said. "Next time you'll get paid up front."

I was so happy Chava was going to be okay I didn't comment on her little dig.

Besides, she was right.

"Before I forget, I brought you a little present," I said, reaching into my bag.

"You shouldn't have," Chava said, "but I'm glad you did." She reached out for the little package I'd brought her.

While she might look frail with her crazy hospital bed hair, a little Aqua Net would fix that, and her hands were strong as she ripped off the ribbon and tore the paper. They were hands that could shuffle cards like a pro, cut my hair, and make excellent pancakes—hands that were a miniature version of my own.

Hands that had raised me, for better or worse.

"Thank you, sweetheart," Chava said waving her new cellphone around. "Just what I wanted!"

She clicked on buttons and scrolled through the features, already comfortable with it, it being the same as mine. I could tell when she got to contacts because her eyes went wide and her face split into a grin.

I'd programmed my own cell number in.

"Just in case you need to reach me," I said. "You aren't off the hook though."

"What does that mean?" she asked, eyes wide with an innocent look that would have done Kendra proud.

"Meaning, I want to hear the truth about you and this Rudy and getting kicked out of Vegas."

"Oh, that," Chava said.

"Yes, that," I replied.

The doctor came in at just that moment to give the okay for her to leave the hospital. We loaded her into the wheelchair—bouquets from Iz and me balanced on her lap—while the nurse and I rolled her out to the front of the hospital. I went out to the lot and got my Subaru, newly washed and waxed. I'd even had the interior detailed for the first time in my life—all evidence of Karl Turner's transport in the back fully expunged. A doggie hammock turned the backseat into a safe way to transport my new pal. At some point I had to come up with a name for my fuzzy companion. He looked up from his spot in the back and wagged his tail.

It felt a lot like love.

We got Chava installed in my front seat with her bags and flowers in the back. The sky was bright and sunny, though the air was still cold, so I turned the heater on high.

So many questions remained unanswered, but Cha-Cha and I had all the time in the world. Right now, all I needed to think about was getting her home.

"Ready?" I asked her.

"Ready, Eddie," she said.

"Let's go home … Mom."

Photo by John Ulman

ELENA HARTWELL'S WRITING CAREER BEGAN in the theater, where she also worked as a director, designer, producer, and educator. Productions of her scripts have been performed around the U.S. and abroad, with some of her plays available through Indie Theater Now and New York Theatre Experience, Inc.

She lives in North Bend, Washington, with her husband and their four-legged kids: Polar, Jackson, and Luna. When she's not writing, she loves to spend time playing with her horse, Second Chance, a twelve-year-old Arabian rescued from a kill pen. Just like Detective Parker, it has taken him time to trust again, but he's coming around.

For more information, go to www.elenahartwell.com.